Taxidermist in the Underworld

MARIA DAHVANA HEADLEY

Louis is working in the basement of the museum when the Devil takes him.

"Boy," says the Devil, and Louis looks up from his diorama. A normal-seeming man with a disturbingly full head of hair, and very red lips, neither young nor old.

"Surely you're not speaking to me," Louis says. He's on the Nile, crafting a landscape out of papier-mâché and paint. Each blade of grass is lined in bronze, and each scale of the crocodile's back is polished to a gleam.

"Boy-O," says the Devil, more formally. "I need a stuffer."

"A stuffer?" Louis shudders. He's busy positioning the tiny legs of an extinct lizard.

"A stuffer," says the Devil. "A veritable stuffer."

Louis looks up, exasperated. "That won't be me. I'm the head taxidermist here at the museum. I'm employed. You should place an advertisement," he says. "You might find someone new to the art, a student. Try the hat shops. There ought to be someone with experience in avians. If you'll excuse me, sir."

The Devil leans forward. "It's you I want, Boy-O," he insists. "You're coming with me to hell."

Louis makes a sound, but they're in the basement where no one can hear him. Though the table's covered with toxic powders, arsenical soap, and small blades, none of them are of any use. The Devil simply leans forward, pries open Louis' mouth, and climbs into his skin. The Devil becomes an armature for the flesh that has belonged to Louis his entire life, and then Louis is stuck, pinched against his own ribcage.

"Here we go now," says the Devil, using Louis' voice. "Pack up a nice valise, there, there. I'll return you to life among the living once we've gotten this sorted, Boy-O, but hell's chock-full of pretty little ghosts, and they're going to waste."

"But, what about Carl?" Louis cries, from deep within himself. He's being forced to share his vocal cords with the Devil, and the Devil's voice booms.

"You can leave Carl a note," says the Devil, and so Louis cribs out a message to his lover: *Wait for me, I had to leave town, I won't be gone long, I'll explain, it's something about my soul.*

But it isn't about Louis' soul. It's about the Devil's whimsy.

Discovery:

> *One cannot fill a ghost with sawdust and stuff it until it stands. It will sag and bulge, and after a short time, one will have not a proper mount, but an abomination akin to Frederick's Lion, eyes incorrectly aligned, teeth pushed out like falling fences.*

Ghosts are the prettiest things in hell, and in that way, they're like song-birds, but when it comes to skinning and reassembling them, they're invertebrates. Louis knows that truth, here in his frenzy, attempting to stretch and gentle ghosts onto their forms. No. They refuse him. They collapse, puncture, snag, and tear.

It's nothing Louis could have known coming in, but they're boneless and as such, impossible. Were he allowed to embalm them, or to wet mount, yes, but not traditional taxidermy. The specimens refuse.

He tries clay, a heavy, old-fashioned mounting method, but the skin of ghosts is weightless and the clay shows through. He tries a wire armature, wrapped in wads of cotton, but the structure of the ghost, being rhetorical, refuses to commit to the wire, and just as he gets it stitched into position, it shudders and dissolves, leaving him covered in dust, a needle stabbed into his own thumb and out again the other side.

He sits for a moment, head in his hands, trying to calm himself, counting the hours in the waking world. How many years are passing above him as he sits here, trying to stuff spirits with sawdust? There will be Carl, and Carl will be missing him. Carl will be trimming his mustache shorter, and Carl will find someone new to love. Carl will walk with a swagger and then with a stick, and then Carl will die, and Louis will still be down here in hell, trying to preserve ghosts.

"I simply don't know what to do with this," he says to the curator, and the Devil's eyes glow a sickly greenish-orange.

CLARKESWORLD

OCTOBER 2014 · ISSUE 97

FICTION

NON-FICTION

Neil Clarke: Publisher/Editor-in-Chief
Sean Wallace: Editor
Kate Baker: Non-Fiction Editor/Podcast Director
Gardner Dozois: Reprint Editor

Clarkesworld Magazine (ISSN: 1937-7843) • Issue 97 • October 2014

"I want a collection for my trophy room," says the Devil. "Stuff my ghosts. That's what you're here for, and you're not going back until you've done it, Boy-O."

"I could stuff a demon," says Louis, but it's a faint hope. The Devil will not give him a demon. The Devil only wants ghosts. The Devil has a roomful of tattered old things, and these are the things he wants mounted, properly and in a dignified fashion.

"Lifelike poses," says the Devil, and Louis moans.

Discovery:

> *One cannot stretch the skin of a ghost over a papier-mâché armature, unless one wishes the ghost to dissolve into the Sunday funnies, or whatever the equivalent is here. The ghost will become one with the paper, and the taxidermist will be left raking his own skin with his fingernails, attempting to disengage the ghost from the machine.*

There have, of course, been taxidermists in hell before. The ceiling of hell is decorated with a frozen flock of dodos, and when Louis mentions that dodos notably lacked the power of flight, the Devil says, "The taxidermists here are low rent. As you can see, I needed someone of a higher caliber."

"Where are the good dead taxidermists?" asks Louis.

"The other place," says the Devil bitterly. "Or so I imagine. There's a collector up there too, who claims them, no matter their sins."

Louis considers for a moment the taxidermy of angels, and feels some relief that at least he doesn't have to do that. Though that would be like birds, and he started his career as a milliner. At least birds have skeletons. Presumably angels do too.

"What exactly is in that collection?" he asks the Devil.

"Old souls, mostly," says the Devil, and shrugs. "There's a trophy room up there full of curiosities. I saw it once. Too brightly lit. You could see the seams, for all they pretend that art gets one closer to god. They have a couple of nicely done cherubim, though. I wouldn't mind a cherub, Boy-O, but they never come down here. Best I can get is a hecatoncheir, and you've seen what a mess my previous stuffer made with that."

Louis looks at the hundred-handed man and feels deep pity for the poor taxidermist who had to skin him. Still, even a hecatoncheir has bones. Louis feels more pity for himself.

Before him, a ghost collapses into a globule, and Louis puts his head down on the desk.

Discovery:

One may stitch up the skin of a ghost and then, using a paper straw, gently, gently inflate the ghost with helium.

"That is not stuffed," says the Devil. "That is a balloon."

The ghost in question, sad-eyed and buoyant, bobs over the heads of hell, tied to a string, before eventually leaking and drooping, bent at the waist, a pitiful excuse for a trophy.

Louis sits on the floor of hell, and hugs his knees. Carl will be at supper in white tie. Carl will be drinking champagne with Oscar Wilde. Carl will be happy to be rid of a troublesome lover whose fingernails smell of formalin. He will eat soft-poached eggs and open his beautiful eyes every morning upon the face of someone other than Louis.

Above Louis, the ghost wobbles and shrivels, emitting a hiss of escaping air. None of these ghosts are pretty. This ghost has bulging eyes and pinned-back ears. It was employed scaring vulnerable people to death, but some spiritualist eventually delivered a message to a murderer for it, and then it was appeased, exhausted and able to fade. There's a small metal plaque still to be affixed beneath it. The Devil's collection is diverse, but the ghosts are all like limp pieces of bridal veil left among moths.

Louis looks enviously at the workings of hell, at the way the bony demons move, their spines and chitins, their tusks. He miserably fills a ghost with cotton balls, and watches it soak them. He fills another with smoke, carefully sealing its entrances and exits, but the smoke trickles out through the ghost's tear ducts, and the ghost looks mournfully at Louis.

Louis looks back. "You're not alive," he says. "You haven't been in centuries."

He adjusts the goo of the eyeball, trying to stabilize it with wheat paste. He thinks of Carl's blue eyes, and of what Carl will look like when Carl is dead.

Discovery:

One may attempt to wet mount a ghost in a fashion wherein the ghost is encased in a vat, and the liquid suspending the ghost is tears. One cannot predict the behavior of the ghost once mounted in such a fashion, however, vatted in the liquid of the vale. One can predict that one will continue to cry. One is, after all, in hell.

The ghost's fingers drift against the glass, pressing and then releasing. The ghost somersaults, disintegrating in the saline, falling to pieces and filtering down to the bottom of the vessel. The Devil shakes his head.

"That's not what I'm looking for," says the Devil. "That looks like algae. I want a whimsy. I want my collection to look playful, Boy-O."

Louis looks at the Devil. The Devil smiles at him.

"Whimsies?" says Louis.

This has now become the personal hell of Louis. Of course it has. Personal hells are the Devil's specialty. Louis is a builder of precise dioramas for museum displays. He'd never put a mouse in a hat, nor a lizard in a gown. He would not force a bird to wear a breastplate. All he wants is to make the natural world unnaturally precious. His time in millinery was horrible, watching women leave the shop with birds perched out of context above their eyebrows. Now things are worse. Ghosts do not belong on walls.

He misses Carl. He funnels another tear from his eye and drains it into the vessel, where the remains of the dismal ghost sift downward like coffee grounds.

He pins a ribbon on the head of a ghost, and attempts to hold it up in an excitable pose. This ghost was a Roman senator. It looks wan, and when Louis picks it up, the ghost makes him sneeze. He tries to fill it with hot air, but it catches fire, and floats up toward the dodos. Things end in conflagration, and Louis prostrates himself on the floor of hell and weeps. All around him, demons douse dodos in kerosene. He prays for salvation, pitifully and without hope, as he tries to go to sleep.

When Louis opens his eyes, his toes burning at some infernal flame, his skin parched, Carl is kneeling beside him, all blue-eyed calm, white suit, and lilac corsage.

"Louis," says Carl, and shakes him. "Step lively. I've come to take you home."

Louis sits halfway up, panicked with relief, and then becomes convinced that Carl is a ghost. Louis grabs Carl's hand, and feels it in its glove, the softness of the moleskin. He looks around for The Devil. The Devil isn't visible.

"Carl?" he says.

"Of course," says Carl. "Did you think I'd let you sell your soul?"

"I didn't sell my soul," says Louis, despairing. "I don't believe in souls. I don't believe in Satan. I don't believe in God. Carl, you know who I am. I believe in science. How did I end up in the underworld? How did you?"

"It was a fuss to get here," Carl says. "There's no train to this part of hell anymore."

Louis looks at him, bewildered. When has Carl ever been to hell? To Louis' knowledge, he's never even been to church.

"The Devil has a pneumatic tube," Louis says. "Not that that helps me. I have to taxidermy all these ghosts, and you don't know what I'm going through."

Carl picks up a limp ghost, and dandles it on his arm. The ghost unfurls like a shirt.

"What's the difficulty, here, Louis?" says Carl. "This seems like it could be posed."

Louis looks at the ghost, unrumpled, smooth and peaceful. The ghost seems soothed by Carl. Carl runs a hand over Louis' forehead and Louis feels the same. His mind twinges with suspicion, however.

"How'd you get here, Carl?" says Louis. "How'd you know where I was?"

"I took a carriage with some white horses," says Carl, and shrugs. "It came to my building."

Louis touches Carl's cheek and it feels cool. He looks into Carl's eyes and Carl looks like his love. Carl moves to kiss him, and Louis finds himself lurching forward with a desperate hunger, and then wonders if *he* has become the Devil, if he is trying to dive into the divine, to become the armature that makes Carl move. He leans back.

Carl kisses him anyway. He tastes like mint. "Don't worry, Louis," Carl says. "I'm here now."

Louis lets Carl help him to his feet, feeling their burnt bottoms crisp. His fingers are like claws and they snag on Carl's suit. He nearly sobs.

"What did you sell to get here, Carl?"

"Try to calm down, Louis, dear. They just let me in," says Carl, and Louis looks at him for a moment, trying not to wonder.

Discovery:

One must ask a ghost's permission before one uses the knives and flenses. One must inquire as to the ghost's preferred method. If one does not, a ghost may convert into a pool of impossible ideas, or mutate into a lady's chiffon burnoose. One must steam and press the ghost, and then pat the ghost into position. One must pet the ghost and pose it, and one must not disregard the ghost's opinions, or one will risk ghost venom dribbled from tentacles, as well as luminous toxins, barbs, and boneless slither. No one wants to insult a ghost. One should have known that much.

Carl strokes the cheek of the newly mounted ghost, the papier-mâché invisible beneath its skin. Louis hammers in the plaque. "*Fever Haint,*" it reads. "*Virginia.*" The ghost raises a hand to its mouth, and screams a pale yellow silence, its body dissolving into tendrils.

"This is lovely work," says Carl, as Louis assesses the heap of half-skinned ghosts before him. Carl has a glow about him, a hygiene that is the antithesis of hell.

Carl may be something other than Carl.

Louis mounts the ghost of a wooly mammoth. He cannot fathom why there was ever a wooly mammoth in hell, but it is a wooly mammoth hybridized to an amoeba, and as such, it drifts about the room, its fur and temper turned to plasma, and it has to be coaxed by Carl to allow sawdust into its seams. Elsewhere, Louis has taxidermied a jellyfish ghost ship found unanchored in the Atlantic and filled with bodies. Each of these bodies required its own negotiation. He has taxidermied the ghost remains of the goddess Echidna, though he was unable to tell what exactly she was until Carl shook out the moths from her folds. Part snake, part woman, a flesh eater and mother of gods, until thousands of years of underworld took her from amongst the cannibals and drew her into a hunger strike.

"A perfectly stunning drakaina, yes you are," says Carl, stroking Echidna's dragon tail, and Louis looks up at him, and feels anxious. Carl has not historically possessed knowledge of mythology, nor of anything, in truth, beyond cocktails and cravats. Carl has always been beautiful beyond his other skills. Louis, he now realizes, has underestimated his beloved.

It is Carl who has touched up the paint on the faces of the ghosts, Carl who has sculpted the ghost dioramas, Carl who has patiently leaned in and dabbed at sagging specters. It is Carl who possesses an encyclopedic knowledge of the levels of hell, Carl who periodically takes a sip of a fizzing drink a demon brought him.

It is Carl who is an honored guest in the underworld.

It is Carl who now makes Louis anxious. His beauty has long seemed unholy, but at home there was no reason to wonder.

7

"Have you been here before, Carl?"

"To hell?" asks Carl, and smiles. "Of course, Louis. Everyone who's anyone has been to hell."

Louis hesitates. "Do you happen to be *from* here?"

"Not at all," says Carl, and Louis thinks of how he's never met Carl's family. He hadn't expected to meet them, of course. He knew one day Carl would marry, and then, perhaps, at a tremendous Southern wedding, he might sit beside Carl's mother and toast her with a julep. Does Carl have parents at all?

"You've spent time here, then? Why didn't you ever tell me?" Louis has a piece of a tremendous lizard in his hands now, just the foot, as he attempts fruitlessly to position its tiny forearms and gigantic haunches. Draped over one shoulder, he's got a limp philosopher, and over the other a three-headed dog.

"I didn't think you needed to know," says Carl, calmly. "Hell was my Thursday evening for a time."

"Was this Oscar?" asks Louis, forlorn. "Did Oscar introduce you to him?"

"Oscar doesn't know the Devil," says Carl. "Oscar goes the other way. The Devil and I go way back, Louis. We've known each other for years."

The Devil strolls into the room, looking pleasant, despite the bat wings that flutter about his shoulders.

"Carl!" he says, and opens his arms. "We've missed you down here. You're looking well."

"As are you," says Carl, and they embrace with the certainty of every set of old lovers since the beginning of time.

Louis watches, despair rising like water in a basement, covering over his memorabilia, drowning the steamer trunks of his ancestors, moldering his heirlooms. He silently laments as the Devil and Carl hold one another, leaning back to look into each other's faces. He thinks about how the Devil always calls him Boy-O.

"I can't believe you never told me," he says to Carl, and Carl shrugs.

"Almost no one knows everything about anyone else," he says. "Even the people they love. There are lacunae, and there are lies: these are the basic ones."

The Devil nods in solidarity.

But Louis imagined he knew Carl. He's spent his career removing the inner workings of animals, and filling them up with other things. If anyone knows everything about a creature, it is Louis. He now knows the soft machinery of all the ghosts in hell, and yet Carl is a mystery.

"I'm sure you understand why I had to bring you down here," says the Devil. "Carl stopped returning my telegrams."

"We didn't end well, the Devil and I," says Carl.

"No one does with me," says the Devil, with some regret. "I tried to apologize, but I'd gone too far."

Louis stitches up the belly of the last ghost with fierce, tugging stitches. He looks up at Carl, who is petting the Devil's cheek.

"Who are you?" Louis asks his lover. "Who even are you?"

The ghost Louis is holding begins to disintegrate, and Louis strokes its seams. "Stay," he says. He hammers its plaque in. "*Swamp Nightmare*," it reads. "*Louisiana*."

Carl is glowing more brilliantly. He's a blue-eyed carnival. A variety of demons come to observe. Louis can see their little pitchers of accelerants. He readies himself to defend Carl, though all he has is a needle and thread.

"No," the Devil intercedes with his minions. "Not Carl. Carl isn't for the flames today."

"I don't mind, if it makes you feel better," says Carl. "Flames have never bothered me."

"I needn't see you burn again, dear one," says the Devil, and sighs. "Once was enough." The demons back away, disappointed. The air smells of burnt feathers.

"How is your collection coming?" the Devil asks Carl, tentatively. "I think of it sometimes. I think of your seraph and your little flock of ophanim in particular. All those beautiful eyes spinning on their wheels."

Discovery:

> *One may, when falling in with God, miss the point. God, after all, would not, by common reckoning, be comfortable reclined across a bed in a small and tidy flat, drinking strong tea. God may not possess a navel, but that would be less than troubling, if one were a taxidermist and used to the beautiful oddities of nature. God may make love like an angel. God may make a man scream in disbelief. God may startle the Devil into saying 'darling' and 'dearest.'*

The Devil and Carl go off into one of the back rooms of hell, and Louis waits. When Carl emerges, he's wiping tears from his face, and when the Devil emerges, he is smiling bravely, abandoned again in the Underworld.

"Boy-O," says the Devil. "Looks like Carl wants you up there."

Louis looks around at the perfectly mounted hydra ghost, at the jellied mold of Dante, labeled simply "*Cartographer*," at the feathered phoenix *ignitus interruptus*.

"Does this mean I'm dying?" asks Louis. He's only 28. At the museum he was in the middle of the Nile, and next, it would have been wild game, a particularly nice and nearly intact lion skin acquired from a dowager.

"Dying isn't such an awful thing," says Carl, comforting him.

"Dying is just a pneumatic tube," says the Devil. "One goes up, one down."

"Does this mean I'm *dead*?" asks Louis.

"You're in demand," says Carl. "Look at your work."

Louis looks down at his stomach instead, checking for a seam. There is none. "Am I an angel?"

"You'll be the official taxidermist. There are privileges to your position," says Carl. "I'm offering you your dream job, Louis."

Discovery:

> *Job Description: All things bright and beautiful may be the aim of the collection, but one may, when falling in with God, never realize that one is being interviewed. God, all Alpha and Omega, all open-armed and bare-chested in one's bed, may never be discovered to be a collector on hiatus from his curation. Nature contains the tentacle and the thorn, the tusk, the membrane, the perfect dusty fish scales of butterfly wings. Nature contains the kissed, the loved and the employed, the insects. Heaven's inhabitants may only be examples of everything that has ever existed on Earth. A taxidermist in heaven must stitch and stuff, smooth and arrange. Sometimes he may return to the bed of the curator, and stay there a century, drifting in a sea of feathered reckoning. Then will he return to the eternal skinning and sewing of souls. Compensation commensurate to experience.*

Louis takes a moment.

"What if you die?" Louis says, and then points at the Devil. "What if *he* does?"

"Then you preserve Carl and put Carl in the collection," says the Devil. "Or me, for that matter. One day. You never know. I prefer a barbed wire armature."

"I like papier-mâché," says Carl, "though if it's available you might be better served by making an armature of spun glass."

"If you're kind, you'll bring me up to the higher place for display, Boy-O, when I go," says the Devil, and then he passes Louis his valise, and kisses him on the cheek in the prickly way one kisses the lover of one's love.

A little scrap of ghost hangs out of the bag, and Louis tucks it in. If it is so ambitious, it deserves to ascend. He follows Carl into the pneumatic capsule, and then, with shocking speed, the great winds of heaven pull them up, and up, from beneath the skin of the Earth and into the vault of the sky.

ABOUT THE AUTHOR

Maria Dahvana Headley is the author of the upcoming young adult skyship novel *Magonia* from HarperCollins, the dark fantasy/alt-history novel *Queen of Kings*, the internationally bestselling memoir *The Year of Yes*, and *The End of the Sentence*, a novella co-written with Kat Howard, from Subterranean. With Neil Gaiman, she is the New York Times-bestselling co-editor of the monster anthology *Unnatural Creatures*, benefitting 826DC. Her Nebula and Shirley Jackson award-nominated short fiction has recently appeared on *Tor.com*, and in *The Toast, Lightspeed, Nightmare, Apex, The Journal of Unlikely Entomology, Subterranean Online, Glitter & Mayhem* and Jurassic London's *The Lowest Heaven* and *The Book of the Dead*, and will soon appear in *Uncanny, Shimmer*, and more. It's anthologized in the 2013 and 2014 editions of Rich Horton's *The Year's Best Fantasy & Science Fiction*, and Paula Guran's *2013 The Year's Best Dark Fantasy & Horror*, in *The Year's Best Weird Volume 1*, ed. Laird Barron, and in *Wastelands, Vol 2*, among others. She grew up in rural Idaho on a survivalist sled-dog ranch, spent part of her 20's as a pirate negotiator and ship marketer in the maritime industry, and now lives in Brooklyn in an apartment shared with a seven-foot-long stuffed crocodile.

Lovecraft

HELENA BELL

First, a mouth appears. It is four centimeters long, curved along the ridge of the old woman's collarbone. It is lined with small nubs of flesh, which is why Ann calls it a mouth and not a slit, a laceration, a suppurative wound.

From the mouth emerges a baby cthulhu: head, tentacles, wings, short arms covered with a soft, pink fuzz. Then another. And another. The number of them does not matter. The old woman does not move as they move. She does not seem to notice their slithering, nor does she acknowledge the quiet, quick barks in rapid succession as they tumble over each other, biting and scrabbling at their siblings while Ann picks them up with a pair of tongs and drops them, one by one, into the garbage disposal and then turns it on.

When it is over, the mouth closes, the old woman goes about her day, and Ann washes her hands.

Such is the way of things.

Ann met the woman, a middle-aged socialite, while she was studying at the university. She had been asked by a professor to transcribe the oral history of the descendent of one of the school's founders and Ann dutifully recorded the names and dates, the occupations. She included the story of the surgeon who had been accused of practicing his marksmanship on the cadavers in the basement of Charity Hospital. Others she left out:

Well, everyone knows that slavery was awful, but there were some good relationships scattered here and there. My great-grandfather and his manservant were so close; they died within a week of each other.

Ann smiled as the woman showed her the Proteus flag she hung every Mardi Gras from the second floor balcony: a cotton sea of red and white centered by a seahorse wearing a five pronged crown. She nodded as the woman described the dress she had worn (the capped sleeves, the thousands of hand-sewn Swarovski crystals, her furred cape), and the menu at Antoine's for her Queen's Supper.

Somewhere between the description of the main course and the bananas Foster, a small animal fell onto the center of the flag. It spread its wings wide, and hopped once, then twice until the woman folded it up in the thin cloth and bashed it with her balled fists.

Ann did not tell her about the second: the one she spied crawling up the sides of the armoire. How it sat, perched in the left hand corner like a gargoyle, watching as its brother (or sister, Ann was never able to tell) was reduced beneath the woman's hands. How it watched her, pitifully and somehow pityingly, and how Ann felt a tightening in her gut and a tingling in her skin. She felt a kinship with this creature she could not describe; it was beautiful and precious and should be treasured. She did not love it. It was not human and could not be loved, but Ann knew in the marrow of her bones that the creature staring at her was hers to protect. As for the other, she could do nothing.

"Oh," the woman said after. "I do hope I can get the stain out."

Ann helped the woman carefully pour bone and membrane into a plastic bag, tie it, and place it outside next to the recyclables. She agreed to finish the interview the next day, even though there was nothing else Ann needed to know. After the front door closed behind her, she quickly went to the window, following the line of the curtains up and up until she spied the tiny cthulhu hanging upside down like a bat, swaddled in the deep blue silk.

Over the next few days, Ann found many things to examine and catalog for an archive she claimed the university was interested in creating for the family. She pored over photos, letters, the document of formal censure from the New Orleans Surgery Society expelling Dr. C.A. Luzenberg from its ranks. She arrived day after day, at 9 a.m. on the woman's front steps, her notebook in hand, eager to begin the day's work.

Sometimes she glimpsed the cthulhu spying on her from a particularly high perch. But no matter what she did, it never came near enough for Ann to examine it further: to pet it, to make friends with it, to comfort it in its obvious terror. It did not trust Ann, and Ann did not know how to gain its trust. The only thing she could do was wait, and hope.

After they finished with the archive, Ann offered to help the woman organize her other papers and books, and later to help her with her social calendar or event planning. One day, as the two women polished the silver, they spotted the cthulhu hanging from the ceiling medallion, its claws (it had some claws, though their number and location seemed constantly to shift) digging into the white wood, turning its head this way and that to watch them with wide yellow eyes.

"Damn thing won't let me get near," the woman said.

"It must know what you did with the other one," Ann said.

"Other *ones*," the woman corrected. "Have to get them when they first come out. One or two isn't bad, but a few years ago I woke up in the morning to find a room full of them. Tearing up clothes, eating the flowers and artwork, making nests out of the good linens. Three maids quit on me in one week. Finally had to tent the house; told them it was termites."

"Surely not," Ann said, as she walked to the center of the room and cooed, lifting her hand up and offering it as a perch.

"You're not scared of it?" the woman asked.

Ann shook her head. "Why should I be?"

"Because it's monstrous," the woman said. "Evil."

Suddenly, and without warning, the woman's neck opened and three more emerged: each identical to the one above Ann's head. The old woman managed to spear two with salad forks, and yelled at Ann to get the third before it got away. Ann ran to the hearth and picked up a heavy iron poker, and as the woman screamed at her to *get it, get it*, she finally managed to land a blow directly between the creature's wings as it ran across the floor. Later, as she scrubbed the carpet with soap and water, she thought she could feel the other one staring down at her and whispering, "You're just like her, aren't you."

"I'll make it up to you," Ann whispered back.

The woman has never been married. She dated a few boys in college, had been escorted to Le Debut and the Debutante Club by a law student from Connecticut who first gave her a ring from Tiffany's, and then revealed that it had been worn first by someone else.

"My mother said never to wear another girl's engagement ring. It's bad luck."

On Mondays and Thursdays, Ann and the woman drove first to the grocery store on Magazine Street where they had the sandwiches that the woman liked to serve for her bridge club, and then to the smaller store on Prytania, the name of which Ann was never quite sure if she was pronouncing correctly. They filled the basket with fresh fruit and vegetables, one bag of blue runner beans which Ann had never seen the woman cook, and supposed it was just one of those things that southern women liked to store in their pantries. The woman selected her meat and seafood, her preferred juices. After a few weeks Ann realized that the woman bought the same foods, in the same amounts each time, and offered to do the shopping herself, but the woman refused. She liked to walk the aisles, to think about what else she might buy. And sometimes she did buy something new: such as a box of strange, sugary cereal which, had the cashier peered closely, had already been opened and reclosed with the small, lifeless body of a dark-skinned creature hastily stuffed inside.

Ann filled out the checks: date, payee, amount, and the woman signed them in a clear, fluid script:

Mrs. C. A. Luzenberg.

Ann was paid in cash. They had never discussed a salary, or hours, or even the job itself, but on the second Sunday that Ann showed up at the woman's house, she was handed a white envelope with seven crisp hundred dollar bills tucked inside. Later, when Ann was refused admission to the graduate school, the steady employment with Mrs. Luzenberg allowed her to stay another year to better her application. And again the next year, and so on, as each time she told herself that if it was not meant to be, she would move on to something else.

The cthulhu didn't grow very fast. When Ann had been working for the woman for more than three years, it appeared no bigger than the day she'd first seen it.

"Trick of the light," Mrs. Luzenberg said. "You have to learn to learn to measure it differently. It used to like to sleep in the bottom drawer of my secretary, curled up like a snake. It always disappeared before I could catch it there, but yesterday I found him spilling out the sides and his head was stuck." Mrs. Luzenberg always referred to the cthulhus as male; Ann wasn't convinced.

"What did you do?"

"I got some bacon grease and a shoehorn and wedged him out. He cried the whole time of course."

"You just let him out?" Though Ann never helped, she knew Mrs. Luzenberg was still trying to catch or kill him: sticky traps, bug bombs, other forms of poison. Ann had been warned not to eat any food, which was uncovered or unwrapped or open in any way. Ann told herself that she continued to work for Mrs. Luzenberg only to ensure that her cthulhu managed to survive another day.

"I suppose I've gotten used to him," Mrs. Luzenberg said. "Much like you."

The other cthulhus never came out in a predictable or regimented fashion. Sometimes the mouth appeared in the morning, sometimes in the afternoon. There would be three in one day, or a complete absence for a month. Ann asked how Mrs. Luzenberg managed to live with the unpredictability; what steps she had taken in her life to manage such inconveniences.

"I avoid airplanes and submarines," she said. "Almost everything else is workable."

Ann learned to watch for small signs: a twitch beneath the skin, a shift in the woman's mood or the tilt of her head. Sometimes she thought she could detect the slightest change in smell: a sudden burst of citrus against the crisp, sterile air. Sometimes she was correct, pulling back the collar of the woman's shirt as the first indentation appeared, darkening to a bruise before it pulled open and the first smooth, tubular appendage appeared.

More often, she was wrong.

When the cthulhu had grown (to Ann's eyes) to the size of a small dog, it finally allowed Ann to come near. It would sit at Ann's feet and allow her to rub its belly. Eventually Ann decided to fashion a harness and leash out of old bridle leather she'd found in the attic so that she might take it outside for walks in the fresh air. Mrs. Luzenberg helped Ann measure the cthulhu's girth and the space between its wings. She showed Ann how to use the punch and awl, how to braid and stich. She found an old sheepskin rug to pad the pieces, which rubbed near the creature's wings.

"Not perfect, but it will do," they declared when the creature stood before them, the freshly oiled leather pieces falling this way and that.

"If he flies off," Mrs. Luzenberg said, "I'm not sure you won't be carried off with him."

"If he does, he does. If I am, I am."

Ann took him to the cemetery across the street. Though the cthulhu had shown no aggression towards others (not the bridge club, the occasional maid or caterer, the man who had to shoo the cthulhu off the 19th-century French dressing table in the upstairs guest bedroom when he came to appraise it for the insurance company when Mrs. Luzenberg decided she needed a brand new policy), Ann did not feel comfortable taking him around moving cars or the huge groups of tourists who bloated the sidewalks. They wandered among the tombs, Ann reading the names and dates and the cthulhu picking his way carefully among the shifting oak roots, sitting back occasionally on his haunches and rustling his wings when she did not move quickly enough for his liking.

"What's his name?" a man asked.

"Luzenberg," Ann said.

"Strange name for a dog," he said.

Ann nodded. "It would be."

Ann and Luzenberg (for now that he had been named, Ann could think of him as nothing else) continued on their path, and the man followed.

"Would you like a tour?" the man asked, and placed his hand near Ann's elbow as if to guide her.

Luzenberg growled low in his throat, low enough that Ann thought perhaps she had imagined it.

"No thank you," Ann said. "I'm local."

"You don't sound like it," he said.

"Nor do you."

He nodded, smiling. "Rhode Island. Just arrived in the city a few days ago."

Luzenberg slowed his pace, eventually working his way between Ann and the stranger.

"Not sure you'd be a good tour guide," Ann said.

"Probably not."

"Then why did you ask?"

She turned to look at him. He had a long face, like an overstretched egg, and his eyes were set too far apart for her liking. The one thing she admired about him was that he had pulled his hands away, clasping them behind his back so as not to invade her personal space. Or perhaps he feared Luzenberg would bite him. Would Luzenberg bite him? Ann wasn't sure.

He shrugged. "I just wanted to talk to you."

"Mission accomplished," she said. "Now if you'll excuse me," and she turned on her heels and walked away. He didn't follow. Another point in his favor.

When she told Mrs. Luzenberg, the latter chided her for being impolite to a stranger in their city.

"He was just hoping to make friends," Mrs. Luzenberg said. "Don't want him to go home with a bad impression of our hospitality." Mrs. Luzenberg then told her a story of how when she was a young girl at Sacred Heart, she and her friends were asked by the nuns to go down to the Quarter where the French Naval Officers were visiting. "It's our responsibility, as hosts," she said.

Ann wasn't so sure, but Luzenberg liked the cemetery so every day for a week she took him. Sometimes they saw the egg-faced man, and he waved at them, respectfully, from a distance. The third time he waved, she noticed he was following behind a tour group, listening as the guide spoke of water tables and storms and caskets floating down the avenue. The stories were all a bit overdramatic for Ann's tastes. A body dies; it is moved to a location suited for a long internment suited to the geological and geographical complexities of the area. To ogle, to take pictures and ask questions about such a private time in a body's life, felt like an invasion.

On the eighth day, the man came up to Ann as she sat reading a book in the shade of one of the crypts. Luzenberg scrambled up the walls to better sun himself, or perhaps to give her some privacy.

"Should he be up there?" the man asked.

Ann ignored him.

"I mean, wouldn't the family mind?"

Ann looked around at other tombs: cracks in the walls and weeds. Bird shit dried and caked into the cement. Some were cleaner than others, owned by families who took more care to preserve their dead. "It's his tomb, in a way," she said, and pointed at the neatly carved names on the marble slab above her head.

Clement.

King.

Luzenberg.

"Oh," he said. "You really are local."

Ann shrugged. "More or less."

"Would you mind giving *me* a tour, then?"

Ann closed her book and looked up at him. From below, his head no longer looked long and stretched. His eyes, she thought, were not so small and beady as before. Above her a shadow loomed and there was a moment of cold silence before Luzenberg jumped down beside her. He didn't growl; he didn't bite. He merely turned his head, tentacles quivering in a questioning manner.

"Why not," she said.

"I'm Howard," he said, extending his hand to help her up.

"Ann," she said.

Howard's vacation extended a week, then a month, then two. Ann gave him Mrs. Luzenberg's address and phone number as her own, and later moved in to the large house to make it easier when Howard came to pick her up. Mrs. Luzenberg insisted that he come in each time to have a drink (no matter the hour) and talk about the weather while Ann finished dressing or fixing her hair or face. Howard assumed Ann was Mrs. Luzenberg's daughter, and neither corrected him.

"It's true enough," Mrs. Luzenberg said later.

Ann and Howard went to the zoo, the aquarium, and the opera. He took her to dinner at a different restaurant each week, claiming he wanted to experience as much of the city as possible before returning home.

Mrs. Luzenberg did not press for details, but gave knowing looks when Ann decided to fix her hair differently, or came home with a new dress to replace the faded and frayed one.

"It's not for him," Ann said. "It's for me. I'm not sure I even like him that much, besides."

"Neither of us is getting any younger," Mrs. Luzenberg said.

Ultimately, Ann believed, Howard preferred her company when they could bring Luzenberg. And truthfully, so did she. With Luzenberg, there was a friend between them, someone they could both discuss and revel in the familiarity. They took him on long walks along the levy, and drove out to the bayou. As winter approached, he even asked her what Mardi Gras costume she had planned for him.

"Cerberus perhaps," she said.

"Isn't that a bit easy? I think we should—" he continued, but Ann wasn't listening.

We, he had said. Mardi Gras would be nine months from their first date. Did that mean something? Did she want it to?

Mrs. Luzenberg insisted it did, insisted that it had gone on long enough for her liking without a kind of understanding. Again Ann mused aloud that perhaps she didn't want it to go on any more. Perhaps she should apply again for grad school.

"Oh Ann, but it's been years since you stopped talking about that. You've been so happy; don't spoil it," and Mrs. Luzenberg poked and prodded Ann's stomach to get her to twirl and show off the new dress that had been bought for her. "You look gorgeous," she said, stressing the word as if surprised to find it so.

Ann and Howard continued on. Ann tried to speak only of easy things: books, movies, plays. Ann cared little for politics, but enough to know that she and Howard disagreed on almost every point. He made her cross the street whenever they were approached by certain people and encouraged Luzenberg to growl at anyone unfamiliar.

When Ann again expressed her intention to finally end things to Mrs. Luzenberg, she was encouraged to give it a few more days as Mrs. Luzenberg had already arranged for them to be invited to the Proteus ball. Ann told herself that it would be an unusual experience, one worth examining from a historical and sociological perspective, something she could discuss in a graduate school application essay, and agreed.

And when Howard arrived to pick them up, even Ann agreed that he looked marvelous in tails.

"This is what this city is about," Howard said, waving his hand at the red and gold silks which hung from the walls, the men in masks and supple leather boots, the girls in their long white dresses and gloves. "This is civilization."

As they danced, Howard's hand held her firm at the small of her back. Her feet ached, and her head swam from the whiskey sours they had given her. Yet all she could think about was how lovely Luzenberg would look nestled in the giant seashell, his wings spread high and wide, eclipsing Proteus with his young debutante queen. Then she thought of Luzenberg's first brother, the crushed entrails smeared between the seahorse and the crown, the redness of her hands whenever she needed to clean the garbage disposal, and her head swam too much for her to bear.

The next day Howard arrived with a large bundle: a rich wool suit expertly tailored (it appeared) for a creature of indeterminate size and wingspan. When he shook it out, Ann realized the pockets had been stuffed with $100 bills. It even came with a cream silk tie covered in small, outstretched hands.

"Do you get it?" Howard said. "He's Ray Nagin. Or Bill Jefferson. They're all the same anyway."

Who is all the same, Ann wanted to ask, but her head pounded, and she thought she felt sick. She couldn't remember drinking as much as she apparently had.

"I don't think—" she started, and then she had to sprint for the powder room.

"Perhaps you should take Luzenberg yourself, Howie. I don't think our Ann is up for it."

When Ann opened her eyes again, she was leaning against the toilet, the old woman's hand in her hair, pulling it back.

"I think I made a mistake," she said.

"We all do, from time to time," Mrs. Luzenberg said. "Next time you'll know better how to control yourself."

"That's not—"

"Shh now, don't exert yourself."

There was a burst of citrus on her tongue, and she looked up at the old woman's neck but it was white and pale and smooth.

Howard didn't come back that afternoon, nor the next day. He had made a dinner reservation for Thursday, a date Ann began to look forward to as a way to break up with him once and for all, but he canceled at the last minute. A man delivered a bottle of expensive bourbon to the house addressed to both Ann and Mrs. Luzenberg. Attached was a note: "With my apologies for missing you tonight. I thought of sending flowers, but thought this was more appropriate. —H"

"He didn't say anything about Luzenberg," Ann said.

"I'm sure he's alright."

Ann called him, but there was no answer. She tried again and again but still was unable to reach him. At night she let the window open in case Luzenberg found his way back to her, and twice she went down to the police station to report a theft, or kidnapping, but whenever they asked her to describe her missing pet (which, they reminded her, was not a police concern), she could tell them nothing. The words would not come. "Try the shelters," they said, and ushered her out the door.

By week three she knew that Luzenberg was gone for good. Mrs. Luzenberg patted her back and said that men were only ever after one thing, and Ann was better off without them. "In a few more years, you can change your name. Everyone will assume you're simply a widow. No one will be the wiser."

Mrs. Luzenberg's neck moved with her lips and Ann held out her hand, letting the small, weak creature fall onto her palm with a slick plopping sound. Both of its eyes were open and it stared at her, unblinking and unafraid. Ann grasped it by the legs, and with a deft snap of her wrist, cracked its head open against the white porcelain sink.

"You never told me why it happens," Ann said.

"Just as my mother never told me," Mrs. Luzenberg said. "Some things are not for us to understand, but to accept, and deal with, and clean up after."

"Doesn't seem fair."

The next Sunday, Ann joined the bridge club in the living room. She was introduced as Mrs. Luzenberg and everyone assumed that she was the widow of Mrs. Luzenberg Senior's son, the one who died in a war. They told Ann how lovely it was that she decided to stay in New Orleans, despite the sad memories, just to care for her mother-in-law. Ann nodded and poured tea from the silver service, crinkling her nose at the faint smell of polish.

After, as they scrubbed the plates and put away the leftover sandwiches in glass containers, poured out the remaining Champagne (it doesn't keep) and folded up the linens, Ann asked why the women hadn't recognized her as Mrs. Luzenberg's assistant.

"We've all been there, dear," she said. "Some women don't get married, and isn't it a shame when their time runs out."

"So they all know the truth," Ann said. "And pretend otherwise."

"Such is the way of things."

"I could still leave," Ann said.

Mrs. Luzenberg turned. The skin of her face was caked thick with makeup, and her neck sagged and jiggled as she moved. Ann could see the definition of her bones and veins as she pulled a dishcloth across a plate. The skin at her neck was pale and translucent and Ann marveled that Mrs. Luzenberg did not die each time a new baby cthulhu pierced through her neck. "You could," she said.

A few years later as Ann finalized the arrangements for Mrs. Luzenberg's funeral, she received a card in the mail. At first she assumed it was yet another note expressing sincere and heartfelt condolences and she set it aside with the others. But when she sorted through them again, she noticed it was unsigned with no return address. Yet the postmark of Providence told her enough. She didn't know which of them had sent it. She didn't think it mattered.

She set the card on the table and considered it for a long time. She could burn it. Or simply throw it away. But when she reached for it, she found her hands folding it into a paper airplane, a shape she hadn't made since she was a small girl. First in half, then triangles in the corners, and long, straight edges for balance. She folded and folded again as she walked up the stairs to the second floor, then the third, then through the hatch which led to the roof. From there she could see the cemetery, and the top of the Luzenberg crypt where the old woman would soon be buried, and for the first time she wondered if Luzenberg was even the woman's real name. She raised her hand to flick the postcard in the air, to let it sail through the heat and humidity until it landed someplace alone in the dark. It would be a petty revenge, but hers.

She pulled her hand back and then thrust it forward, before back again with the plane still in her hand. She could not let go.

Howard wouldn't have sent a card. He got what he wanted; he was done with her. This was from the other one: her Luzenberg. To let her know that he was all right, and alive, and out there in the world somewhere. As she thought it, the skin at her neck tingled she inhaled the rich scent of citrus.

Smiling, she brought the pointed nose of the cardboard airplane to the skin at her collarbone, digging at the small indentation she knew was beginning to form. She pulled and sawed at it until she could feel her blood pour out of her and a tiny, delicate wing extend. Ann helped the creature out, setting her on the ledge where her wings might dry before reaching for another. She pulled and she tore until the skin at her chest was as loose as a cape and still they kept coming. They rolled out of her, sliding down her legs and summersaulting over their siblings. They barked and they cawed and they butted their heads and entangled their tentacles.

Finally, with the postcard still clutched in her fingers she clambered onto the roof with them, crawling on all fours and leading her parade of cthulhus towards the precipice.

She stood, and the crowd of them, a single organism, leaned against her legs, steadying her as she pulled her arm as far back as it would reach. They flapped their wings in encouragement as she flung the cardboard plane high into the air.

And then they leapt after it.

She watched as they soared over the cemetery, past the dead and the treetops and all the houses where all the Mrs. Luzenbergs of the world lay sleeping. Her chest heaved and flushed and tingled as her skin desperately tried to reknit itself. She pulled it free again and again, reaching into her chest and her liver and her kidneys and the dark spaces in between to pull the last of them free: the timid and the shy and the half-formed and set them upon the air.

Blood and death and life and brutal, hard desire streamed out of her, and still the cardboard airplane sailed. It rose and it rose and it pulled hundreds of cthulhus behind it, to make of the world what they would.

ABOUT THE AUTHOR

Helena Bell is an occasional poet, writer, and international traveler which means that over half of what she says is completely made up, the other half is probably made up, and the third half is about the condition of the roads. She has a BA, an MFA, a JD, and a Tax LLM which fulfills her life long dream of having more letters follow her name than are actually in it. Her work has appeared or is forthcoming in *Shimmer Magazine, Brain Harvest,* and *Rattle.*

Seeking boarder for rm w/ attached bathroom, must be willing to live with ghosts ($500 / Berkeley)

RAHUL KANAKIA

First Listing

I'm looking for a roommate, preferably a gay male, non-drinker, non-drug user, to share a comfortable Craftsman-style, three-bedroom, two-bathroom bungalow in Berkeley. Owner-occupied home has hardwood floors, skylights, fireplace, built-in bar-b-q, nice garden, washer and dryer. Clean and well maintained. Room is approximately one hundred eighty sq. ft and includes attached bathroom.

This is a quiet residential neighborhood, full of children and dogs. You must have your own telephone, but all other utilities shared. Place is wired for DSL. I want to build a comfortable home based on communication and shared responsibility. Share with owner (me), a sixty-one-year-old gay male and small business owner who works in the ectoplasmic removal / storage sector and has lived in the home for thirteen years.

Sole caveat: The living room, garage, basement, and third bedroom are used primarily for ectoplasmic storage. Don't know if you've ever seen them, but ghost flasks are small, unobtrusive, and thoroughly safe. However, mine do emit a slight noise. The previous boarder, a twenty-seven-year-old medical student, is leaving due to excessive emotional involvement with the ghosts, and I'd prefer if my next boarder attempted to leave them alone as much as possible.

The rent is $500.00 per month with a $725.00 deposit.

It's available immediately!

Please reply back to this ad or call 555-658-5109. Leave a message if I'm not at home.

Thanks!

Second Listing

First of all, I'd suggest that potential boarders read this ad in its entirety before responding, because I'm a little bit tired of the look on peoples' faces when they walk in here. I'm completely happy to talk to any and all prospective tenants who wish to come by. I love meeting people and I love shooting the shit. It's just that, well, it's not really very pleasant when a stranger takes one look at your home and then does their best to try to escape.

And I am really tired of people trying to bargain me down by acting like they'd be doing me a favor if they took the room. You know, I understand its somewhat inconvenient to live with ghosts and that's why the rent is *already* fairly low for this area.

But the inconvenience is not huge. If you've never seen a bottled ghost, please be aware that it's nothing like a free-range ghost (which are usually as big as a person, can run a hundred miles per hour, shatter glass with a scream, chill skin with touch, etc). No, during the bottling process, the compression vac solidifies and sluggifies the ghost. Most squash down to a nugget that is only 2" tall and 0.5" thick, and they're kept soaking in a solution that prevents expansion. They can move, and even speak, but only very slowly.

Most ghosts in my home were removed ages ago. They were haunting someone who did not want to be haunted (though you'd be surprised by how many people actually don't mind being haunted). And although I mostly don't go on calls anymore (except for old, trusted clients), I am able to live very well on the small storage fee paid by various hauntees to keep their poltergeists bottled. They say that all ghosts have to do just one last thing before passing on . . . but sometimes that thing is awful inconvenient for those who are left.

Some tenants have asked me whether the ghosts *need* to emit so much noise, or if they can't be silenced somehow. The bottles are high-quality and rated to last for a hundred years. Sometimes they can be a bit noisy, I know. That's because the last tenant riled them up a bit.

However, when I say noisy, I am talking about more of a whisper than a shout. The bottles are thick. When they scream their loudest, they can just barely be heard. I just don't want to be like those big, soulless, ectoplasmic storage companies with their desert warehouses: I would never deprive any person—even a dead person—of his or her voice.

The ghosts are not ordinarily this loud. My last boarder, a medical student who I'll call "Chris," paid perhaps a bit more attention to the ghosts than was merited. After another few months of benign neglect, I believe they will quiet down somewhat.

The problem was that he became too attached to one little fat girl—maybe twelve—who killed herself after being invited to a Facebook group called the *'I Think Cynthia S_____ Is an Ugly B*tch' Society*. Her name happened to be Cynthia S____ and she just joined for a moment, in order to see how many other people were part of it (seems half the school was enrolled). But after joining, a picture was taken of the notification and, by the next day, everyone in school knew Cynthia S_____ had joined her own hate-club.

Chris would go down into the basement with a folding chair and sit in front of the girl's bottle. It was only as tall as the last joint of his thumb, but Chris didn't mind bending down very close in order to hear her shrieks. He'd sit there and not even try to wipe away the tears flowing down his face like lava. I really do think that he *enjoyed* being sad.

Sometimes he would come upstairs and ask me how we could *get* the little bastards who'd tormented CS.

Now, I am not a hard man, but after the umpteenth repetition of this scene, I had to tell Chris, "Let's not pretend like we don't both understand the pleasure of destroying another person."

"What does that mean?" he said.

"It's not a judgment on you," I said. "I just know that I've been in my share of various different sorts of *'I Think Cynthia S_____ Is an Ugly B*tch' Societies*. And I'm sure the same is true of you."

He got silent, as if I had said something startling and cruel. And then he retreated to his room.

I don't go out of my way to speak to the ghosts, myself. It wouldn't be fair or right to ask them to tolerate me. I am not their friend and I'm not their avenging angel. I'm their jailer.

I know this is not an appetizing story. I'm not trying to appetize you. All I am telling you is that, contrary to the insinuations of certain rights groups, some function *is* served by locking away these ghosts. They do have a certain presence to them that, to the wrong person, can be upsetting. However, if you simply leave them be, then you will be completely fine.

If this seems like a livable situation, please call or email. The home is a beautiful, well-maintained three-bedroom Craftsman. The neighborhood is wonderful and safe. The proffered room is large and has an attached bathroom. I'd prefer a gay male, but I'm open to others.

Third Listing

From the recent drop-off in the number of phone calls, I've intuited that many of you have seen a certain libelous listing for my address on the RentrBWare cellphone application. I considered hiring a lawyer to respond to that listing, but I decided against that, because I really do believe that if a person simply expresses himself cogently and clearly, then, if his listeners are right-minded people, they'll sense the truth pouring out of him.

Do I have a certain reserve? Yes. But I would not say that I am "flat of affect" or that I have "a pervasive pattern of detachment from social relationships."

I do not collect ghosts in order to feed "a narcissistic desire for a perpetually captive audience." I do not collect them at all. I store them. And I do so because that is my livelihood.

But I am not pleased by them, and I do not enjoy their company.

In life, I'm sure I would have loved many of my ghosts. They're often fascinating individuals, and they contain much potential for fascinating interaction. For instance, I have a whole shelf of men collected in '84 from SF General's AIDS ward. Chris once interviewed them for a well-received academic paper on patient attitudes re: experimental treatment.

As ghosts, they've been restored to their prime, with their slim moustaches and long bronzed legs. When they were alive, I would've hung around awkwardly at the edge of their orbits and tried to attract a glance from them. In fact, when they were alive, that's what I *did* do. I came to SF out of Rapid City in '67, as soon as I learned that there was a place for people like me. But even when I was eighteen and slim and smooth-skinned, those guys never really liked me. I don't know why. I hung around in the same bars, the same bathhouses. But I never figured out how it was done.

I guess there's just some strangeness coiled up inside of me. There've been times in my life when I would've reached down through my throat and yanked that strangeness right out, if I'd only known what it was.

Still, I suppose that thing is why I am alive, and they are dead.

But I don't cry about it. I'm not lonely. I get out there. That reviewer would have you think I'm some John Wayne Gacy with a crawlspace full of bodies. Far from it! I belong to a vacation club: my choice of forty-six locations—plus reciprocal benefits at other clubs. Almost every month, I'm off somewhere. Every February, it's Tahoe. Every March, it's Hawaii. In August, I usually go to Mexico and see a guy who kind of acts as my boyfriend, when I'm around.

If those men down in my basement could see how that awkward kid turned out, I think they'd be proud of how I've put a life together.

If you live here, you won't be bothered. Honestly, I hardly need a boarder. It's just . . . I have so much in my life. I want to pass things along and help others. That's why the rent is so low, really.

The neighborhood is good. The room is large. The house is airy and clean. Utilities (including Internet) are included. Please call or email. If I don't answer, please leave a message.

Fourth Listing

It's just as I feared. The poster on RentrBWare is none other than my former boarder, "Chris." I had suspected that it might be him. But I had hoped that perhaps it was some business competitor or other less-than-gruntled individual.

Still, this does not in any way alter my position as to the lack of veracity behind Chris' reviews. It is false to its core, and I don't care how much documentary evidence there might be. Those pictures of cockroaches perhaps might've been taken in my house. But the context is entirely missing.

I know that I'm no saint. In my life, I've sometimes succumbed to hatred. But I do my best to hate things that deserve hatred. Like termites. I hate termites. I can *understand* hating termites. Termites damn near hollowed out my ceiling. Termites will bankrupt you and then bring your house down on top of you. But I don't understand hating cockroaches. Do cockroaches come out at night and nibble your face off or something? Because I tell you, I don't think a cockroach has *ever* killed a man. Or a woman, either. Cockroaches are harmless. They just wanna eat your garbage. You don't want cockroaches? Don't be like Chris and let the soy sauce dry out in the black stack of plastic take-out sushi bowls that rises higher and higher on your desk—just cause it's hidden behind your computer monitor doesn't mean the cockroaches can't see it.

Not that I am bothered by mess. I believe you can do whatever you want, so long as you are strong enough to bear up under the consequences of doing that thing. But if you leave out garbage and cockroaches come and eat it, then don't act like *they* are the disgusting menace. And don't act like I'm some monster because I won't let you spray pesticide around like it's perfume. That poison drains into our Bay!

Sometimes I think that the more harmless and defenseless something is, the more people want to destroy it. I swear to God, once I went into someone's house while they were gone and I could not *find* the fucking ghost. I checked between the folds of every evening dress in their walk-in closet and clawed my way down to the bottom of the huge wooden chest full of Legos in their basement rumpus room.

Finally, I gave up and called the homeowners and they said to look in the pool. And there she was, right down at the bottom: almost invisible, because her skin was blue as the water. Only the shimmering of her blonde hair gave her away. When I dived down to get her, she put a finger to her mouth and said, "Don't tell. I need to stay hidden."

When I told this story to Chris, he became agitated. He started pacing back and forth in the kitchen and then he said, "Did you ask what she was hiding from?"

I said, "I was underwater, son."

"But you vacuumed her into your machine."

"Of course I did," I said. "I had to. That's how I pay my mortgage. That's how I live."

He shook his head from side to side, and then he went into his room and slammed the door and put on his headphones and avoided me for ten or fifteen days. Chris was perpetually avoiding me. And if he wasn't avoiding me, he was talking to me about borderline personality disorder or some such nonsense.

Chris never understood that you might be able to pull that crap out of a textbook, but none of it has anything to do with real life. Chris doesn't know shit about the world and how hard it is to find your place in it. That's fine, though. I'm sure I was the same way when I was his age.

Fifth Listing

Room for rent. Room has hardwood floors, plenty of light, and attached bathroom. Utilities (including cable and Internet) are included. House is a wonderful Craftsman-style, three-bedroom, two-bathroom bungalow in Berkeley. $400. Neighborhood is exceedingly safe. Close to Pixar headquarters and a number of fine eating and shopping establishments. Wonderful deal!!! Owner is fifty-seven-year-old professional w/ small business. Stores selected (very safe) ectoplasmic individuals on behalf of families / friends of deceased. Totally up to code. Never had any issues. If interested, please call or email any time! If I don't answer, please leave a message!!!

Sixth Listing

I've had boarders for more than a decade. No complaints. Never. I treat people fairly and I expect that they'll treat me fairly. Some of you . . . I guess I can't blame you. The Internet isn't like the real world. On the net, people aren't honest. But with the emails and calls I got . . . you'd think my last ad was an invitation to come over and get murdered, rather than an honest attempt to inform the public of a perfectly good living situation.

I don't know. Maybe I'm done. Maybe I just won't rent out that room anymore. I don't need the money. I'll move the bottles from the living room into the extra bedroom. I'll be able to watch TV in there again. The ghosts react oddly to TV: they bubble and bulge and press themselves to the edges of their bottles when they see the screen. It agitates them. Normally, they pass their lives in a sort of timeless state. But the flickering of that image shows them that time is passing, and their loves and hates are slowly leaving this world.

There's one in particular that I would like to remove from my living room: it's a baby. I actually have a number of babies on site. For awhile, I specialized in them. They bother most ectoplasmic storage specialists. But not me.

Chris once told me that human beings are hard-wired to feel an "urgent sense of distress" at the crying of a baby. Well, that's not true. You know how many times I've gone down to the Kaiser Hospital over on Howe Street and sucked the ghost of a crying baby out of one of their incubators? Just maybe like two hundred times. Crying babies? That's a Wednesday for me.

But this particular baby is worse than usual. This baby was—is—all turned inside out. Yeah. It's all mottled and red and bloody, with the intestines poking out, and the skin all thick and lumpy on the outside. Looks a bit like a lizard. In the hospital, it cried and cried and cried and cried. I softened it up in a bath of silver nitrate and sucked it right into my holding tank. No problem. It's on my living room mantle.

This baby. I don't know. It was haunting that there neo-natal ward. If I hadn't a taken it out, it'd still be there.

Most of the time, it lays, gasping quietly, on the bottom of its bottle. But when the TV turns on, the baby's misshapen head lolls back and it lets out that shriek from beyond the grave. And I turn and I look at it and listen. And you know why? Because I don't flinch. That's not who I am.

Why did this baby stay behind? What was it supposed to do? What is a little lizard-baby even *capable* of doing? And what will happen to it if it stays on my mantle? The scientists say that ghosts slowly boil away: if they don't accomplish their aim, they lose half their substance every few hundred years. But when does half times half times half equal nothing? We still don't know. We've only been bottling ghosts for fifty years or so. None have yet dwindled away to nothing.

All I know is that I came to this place as a boy. And I had no friends. No lovers. Nothing. No means of surviving. Most of the people who came here at the same time are now dead, but I did not die.

I found a trade. And I practiced it. I built a business, and I bought a house. I took in boarders and I treated them well, and they treated me well. And years passed

I liked Chris. And I think he liked me.

He moved out over such a tiny, simple thing. One morning, we were both in the kitchen. I was making an omelet, and he was brewing coffee. He had his favorite ghost—it was that little girl—sitting on the mantelpiece, and he was smiling at her and telling her about his day. And then I noticed him looking at me with a guilty, furtive look. And I stood up.

He yanked his hand away from the bottle. One quick glance showed that the bottle had been unscrewed a tiny little bit more. Not much. Not enough to let her go. But a few more turns and she'd have been free.

And that's when I decided.

"It's been good having you here," I said.

"The same," he said.

"You . . . you care about the ghosts, don't you? I mean . . . that's why you've stayed so long."

He was clutching one of his hands with the other one. His eyes flickered back and forth, like I'd just bottled him.

"I'll leave them to you," I blurted out. "When I die. I'll leave them to you. In my will. My sister's kids won't want them. You can come here and let them go. It'll take a day or so, but you can let them go. Maybe you could take them out into the woods or something, so they'd have more time to disperse. But you could let them go. I don't know when I'll die. But in twenty years, some of them, maybe, will still be able to do their thing."

"No, don't do that," he said.

"I'll give you the house, too," I said. "By then, it'll be completely paid off."

He looked at the girl. She was beating against the walls of her bottle. And then he looked at his hand. "N—No," he said. "I don't . . . "

"By then, you'll be making a lot of money," I said. "You won't need the storage fees. Right now I need them here. I live off them. Can you imagine what it'd be like for me if I were to let them go? Their next of kin would sue me. I'd go bankrupt. I'd lose my house. But you could do it. I'll work the legal angle so that you're not liable. You won't own them or anything. You won't be legally or morally culpable. All you need to do is come back here. Someday. Maybe twenty or thirty years from now, when you're married and you've adopted three children. It'll just take one day. And I think that after I'm dead, I'd really enjoy knowing that they were free."

He shook his head and told me that he would think about it. Then he went off to his room, leaving the little girl there on the sill.

Three days later, he emailed me his notice. His boyfriend came to move him out.

It was four weeks before I moved that little girl back into the basement.

I don't know why he left. I don't know why he didn't accept the offer. I thought I was giving him everything that he wanted. But I guess I was wrong.

It's true that Chris wasn't the first person to insinuate that there's something wrong with me . . . I don't know. I just don't know.

But I do know that I don't deserve to be alone.

That makes me sound awful needy, but it's the truth. You've gotta sense that. I haven't done anything that merits this kind of exile from humanity. I don't want anything special from you. I don't want you to be my friend or my confidante. I just want to occasionally come home to the sight of another living being.

The room's $400. It's big. It's clean. It's got a bathroom. You won't find a better deal.

Please call (or email). Leave a message if I'm not at home. The reason for that is that the phone's a landline, see? It doesn't register missed calls, like a cellphone does. And if you don't leave a message, I'll never know that you ever even called in the first place.

ABOUT THE AUTHOR _____

Rahul Kanakia's first book, a young adult novel entitled *Enter Title Here* is coming out from Disney-Hyperion in Fall '15. Additionally, he has stories appearing or forthcoming in *Clarkesworld*, *The Indiana Review*, *Apex*, and

Nature. He holds an MFA in Creative Writing from Johns Hopkins, and a B.A. in Economics from Stanford, and used to work in the field of international development. Currently, he lives in Oakland, CA and makes his living as a freelance writer and content creation consultant.

Pithing Needle
E. CATHERINE TOBLER

We have run toward enough danger to understand this is unique, this conflict will change everything we know. It will change the Nessik, too, but we don't care about them in this moment, because hundreds of thousands of their young are—

Are eating our—

Blackout.

We came together, armed, prepared, and yet not. They sent an entire division, but it will never be enough. We can see that the moment our cargo ship touches down; everything stands in ruin: charred and smoking trees, satellites drawn down from orbit, the alien ship itself, a crumpled tin-can spire rising six fucking miles into the clouded sky. The rain is ash and not water, not washing clean, but sticking, to our armor, our weapons, to the coiled Nessik bodies that lash out of absolutely nowhere to engulf us.

Swallowed by a thousand tongues, yanked into a quivering mouth with a sharp beak that bites and bites, digested even before the creature even swallows. A hard boot against a soft throat, those thousand tongues pull back, but only for a breath, and then they're back, hauling me deeper until I pull the slick trigger, turn the tongues into mash that streams violet across my goggles, mash that doesn't move until I scrape my fingers through it. The alien (later, the word Nessik comes later) erupts dead at my feet, looking like a vicious neon orange hermit crab turned inside out over its shell.

There's no time to admire—there's another one, tentacles and arms coiling around my boots. This one is hot, nearly steaming in the jungle humidity. The heat bleeds straight through armor, causing me to think my boots are melting. I look and it's time enough for the Nessik to yank me off my feet entirely and haul me in. Back into a mouth that looks like the first mouth that looks like a yawning cavern of death. But I'm not going down that way. I could pull this trigger all day.

So I do.

They never stop. I can't count how many there are; the crashed ship, rising six miles into the clouded sky, seems as though it will never empty. I can't count the numbers, but I do notice the differences among them. There are larger aliens and smaller aliens—it's the smaller ones that give me pause—not because they're potentially juveniles (children have ceased to matter in this world—who would bring a child into this ruined world? Who?), but because they outnumber the larger aliens. I see how some of the smaller aliens are marked; deep grooves raked into their shells, like someone cut them with a blade; sooty streaks where they were scorched with fire.

This thing that rises in me might have a name; someone might call it sympathy. I call it bullshit. Curiosity if anything else, because when a thing falls from the stars—they called it the Arecibo Event, having no idea what the ship held, what it was doing as it plummeted from the sky and into the ground at Arecibo—I wonder what the fuck it is, what the fuck it contains. I wonder because I know I'm about to be in the middle of it.

They never stop, these monsters. The ground is alive with them; incessant, a kind of black-oil ocean dredged from deepest space to swallow the land as we once knew it. They are like nothing I have seen—maybe in childhood, for I remember hermit crabs, legs protruding from a stolen shell, but these aliens are more perfect than that; their shells are not stolen, they are absolutely part of their shells, flesh and shell as one thing. Writhing arms and tentacles emerge from these shells—there is the impression of a face, but there are no eyes and I wonder how they see, how they find me every single time I escape. I climb a tree—it's on me. I round a boulder, there's another. I crouch under a busted arc of the old Arecibo dish, there's half a dozen of them on me inside thirty seconds. They are relentless, merciless, alien.

I don't try to talk to them—they have mouths but use them only to eat. I will not be eaten—slick trigger in slick glove, I fire the way they eat: constant. Sometimes I get there before they do; sometimes I'm firing and a soldier is already inside that shell, digesting. A thousand tongues inside one hungry, angry mouth.

I never wonder what this is; I know all too well. This is what I signed up for, because there was nothing else. The world changed long before I was born, swallowed by water and scorched by sun—and this will only change it more. This is all there is now. Writhing ground, falling sky, and I love it.

I'm also good at it. I've been spliced twice at this point—twice or more, everything fades under continued augmentation (but for you, you never fade). I suppose I am not entirely human anymore. I can see better, move better, but no one down here cares (until they discover it, until they do). The tentacles that wrap me up and haul me into a mouth don't care (until they do).

We reach the ship days later. The sky tells us it has been only hours, but surely it's days we've been hacking and shooting and sliding through the muck of exploded alien bodies. They litter the landscape; the dead outnumber the living here, the living aliens moving on, spreading through the jungle as they devour. More divisions arrive to greet them, while we lumber toward the ship.

It's the strangest thing we've never seen; it looks like a hive, which is what we come to call it. You never kick a hive because of what may come boiling out, but when the troops place the explosives in an effort to bring the upper levels of the thing down, they only succeed in busting open all the levels that weren't broken open upon landing. This ship explodes with life; aliens everywhere.

Slick and click, I could do this all day, until one of the smaller aliens gets the jump on me. I see it in your face a second before it happens; the widening of your eyes before the alien snatches me. It hauls me backward *hard*, so hard I'm wedged inside its mouth with my rifle parallel to its beak. I can't reach the trigger, so spin the rifle like I'm performing a drill, in a perfect line before a review committee. The rifle doesn't spin, is clocked by a thick tentacle that wraps it, flings it. You catch my spit-slick rifle and then I'm gone—swallowed by a black mouth.

There is no direction here; I can say down is down because I've been swallowed, but there's absolutely no light, no sense of motion outside the muscle that contracts around me as it swallows, draws me in. Warm, slick muscle ripples around me with such strength I can't move against it. I try, but I can't turn. I can't wriggle my way up or down. The scream that rips out of me is silenced by the slither of wet muscle across my neck, my mouth. This alien tastes like salt.

And then—

Violent light as I am spat from the maw, into a room that has no corners, no edges. I slide across what feels like half-warm wax, unable to gain any purchase. The room terminates in a soft cup; this cradles me and is strangely comforting after the black suck of muscle. The alien that swallowed me perches on the rim of this room, screaming. Eventually, this alien begins to calm and the scream turns into a chitter turns into a pattern, a pattern that my brain begins to dissect.

Language is patterns, repetitions; pauses and stops and resumptions, and this, *this* is what the alien is doing. It's talking to me. Trying to tell me something. I understand none of the words, but the structure becomes familiar. The alien repeats itself, clicking, and then there are two aliens, and three, and more. They have no eyes, but they absolutely watch me as I drip saliva and mud into the cup of this room.

There are no edges in the room and I cannot stand up on the flexible, waxy floor; I can only sprawl, watching them as they watch me. The alien who swallowed me becomes indistinct from the others on the lip of the room; they all swallowed me, they all scream at me, over and over, fucking—

One slides into the room with me, all mouth and fury, still screaming. The fury is familiar if not the words, and I scream back, refusing to draw myself into a ball as the alien nears me; I should, should make myself as small as possible. But I lash out.

The strange thing is—the strangest amid a tableau of strange—is that the alien allows it. It takes my punch as my fist strikes its leading tentacle. Endures the way I kick its shell as it slides toward me. The alien spins under the impact, also unable to hold onto anything in this room. This *cell*.

It's a cell—me a prisoner, but if the alien can't move here, was the alien also held here? Its shell is marked, five long scratches near what I take for its mouth. But as it spins, I see more. Five becomes fifteen becomes twenty and more. Were it human, I would take the marks for years, but it's not and I don't.

It lets me beat on it, until I realize I'm not getting anywhere; the weight of the alien pulls the flexible cup on which we fight down and down. It provides no support, no surface from which to attack, so at long last we can only both sprawl there, heaving with exhausted breath. I stare at the thing: black-oil ocean waiting to flood over me. It is never still, tentacles and arms rippling even as it does not reach for me. The weight of its shell presses the waxy cell flatter than my body did on its own; I stretch, meaning to find a way up and out, but the cell gives every time I move, and there won't be any walking up these walls.

Bees could live here, I think, but even bees have straight-edged walls.

I do not sleep and if the alien does, I am unaware of it. It never stops moving.

At some point, it begins chirping at me again. Slow, precise. It chirps a sequence of four sounds. And again. When it comes again, I think I might go mad from it, but I've been spliced, am part machine.

I open my mouth and repeat the sequence as given; it is only mimicry. The alien flinches, scrambles and tries to get away, but there is nowhere to go. The panicked action leaves us rolling together, the flexible wax cell moving with us. It is like being trapped on a boat with a very large animal, only unable to jump overboard into cleansing waters. I dig my hands into the floor-wall, but cannot break through the material. It is impossibly strong.

The aliens on the lip of the room screech at the alien nearer to me. The alien calms and chitters at me again. I don't know the words, but my augmented throat appears able to make these sounds, so I repeat them again. Again, the alien seems to panic—screaming like comets across the black sky—and this time, the lashing is so forceful, I am swept back into tentacles, pulled into its dripping mouth.

Beyond.

The pithing needle, born deep inside the alien, pierces the base of my brain, splicing through bone and tissue. There should be only black—only death—but it's a riot of colors and scents that I have never seen or smelled before. It's not green and it's not grass, but it's alive and writhing and under my feet, sliding up my calves with a texture like knives, coiling around me like it knows me. It's not blue or orange; it's not lemon or onyx; it's deeper than any of these things as humans know them. It's a flexible floor, never moving because in space in there is no up or down. It's bodies forced into breeding cells until none can move without stirring the entire cell to chaos. It is eating one's way to the bottom until one is at the bottom and is slowly eaten in turn. Endless mouths, teeth all the way down, needle rattled in skull.

Confinement. A hundred thousand bodies pressed together; I understand this in a way that comes without words. The sensation of being there floods through me; no longer remotely human, me, but alien. Coiled into shell, tentacles whipping to gain space, but there is never space, not even when another cell manages to burst loose, eating their own kind, stacking shells mortared with the dead so they may slither out, to spark an engine overload, to toss this prison ship from the stars. No words; I smell every second of confinement, taste it in the back of my throat, until it gags me, until—

The solid crunch of the alien's shell as it shatters. Gray slop, and razor-sharp jackknife shell pieces carving into my armor. We are hauled from the cell by the other aliens with impossibly long tentacles that have broken through the juvenile's shell, have shattered it to retrieve me, wet and dripping as a newborn. New eyes, new fingers, new everything.

They fling me from the ship, into the chaos beyond. I land gracelessly in the mud—full on rain now, always rain, pulling ash from the sky above the burning city. The landscape moves; it isn't the storm, but the aliens as they move ever away from the crash site, as they explore Earth as invader, colonist, glutton. They do not slow, even as military divisions drop from the sky, even as drones circle from above. The coastal water writhes with their black-oil bodies, but light fractures my view; human soldiers drop around me. Some stay to haul me to what they perceive as safety.

The rain feels like blood running out of me. I lift a hand to the back of my neck—there should be a hole, evidence of the violation, but there is nothing. Nothing. They cradle me (flexible wax, cannot gain purchase), fingers probing, seeking. What was done, can I see them, am I here? So many questions, but every answer comes out in the alien's own tongue. I chitter, I warble, I send streams of echolocation up and into the storm.

This is alien sight—I am looking at my commander's face, framed by the burning tree above us, but I see the far distant aliens. They move like a tsunami of black water; they do not pause, they overrun every city they encounter. The sky is full of military—I ping these sounds so that I might see off the helicopters, off the rappel lines, off every rifle and every weapon I know will not matter. Small stands will be made, but these aliens are hungry—they have been held (sagging cell, flexible, too much weight and too many mouths and oh eat me so this will cease) and will be held no more. They revel under these rainy skies; every droplet of rain echoes back to me, flooding like the aliens—the *Nessik*! A name, a people, a place they have come from. I reach into the collective—so many, I still cannot count them—and I see a black world, a world that never stops moving, because they are the ground, are the water, are the sky.

What did they do to me?

Unknown?

Too many—factors.

Too many Nessik.

I chitter. They stare. I cannot form the proper words to tell them, about the ship and the cells, and then you are there, cradling my head, asking if I can see you.

I see you, in more colors than ever before. The color that glosses your rain-wet face has no word; the taste of the rain that slides from your nose and into my chittering mouth has no name on this world. What world—this world, but I cannot say where I am. I could reach into the drone that passes over us, could crack open the housing and show you the spill of wires, connective pathways; I could turn these colors and tastepaths into a map, could pull you inside this space and show you, but you would only ever know a fraction—a fragment, a—

The drone slows above us; its red-slit eye oscillates over me, Cyclops pondering. My breath stutters in my throat—rain still feels like blood and you ask if I can see you, if I can feel you, and your fingers are like burning brands against my neck. There should be a print, a mark to make your passage evident, but these marks are better buried. Your goggles light up in drone-red, in Cyclops-fury, and then fades into rain as the drone moves on.

What did they do, you want to know and I cannot say. Cannot form the words; there is rain, and there is the color of your face and the taste of the rain, sliding off of you and into me.

Blackout tastes like sunlight.

Later, in the tent, the rain furious on the meager roof. It will punch through, and this reminds me of something, but I do not know what. Your fingers comb through my wet hair, my eyes slit shut, and you still want to know—you don't even have to ask, because I can hear the unspoken thought—what they did, what did they do, did they—

No. It wasn't—

But I suppose in a way it was. *Pithing.*

You are more than a needle inside of me. As quick as they were— nothing and then there, there where I need you to be. The rain on the tent roof, your fingers on my hips—flexible, pressing, but you can't tear through. My fingers sliding up your neck, into your hair. Pithing. Let me tell you. Jack in. Deeper.

They took me, spliced me so I could understand—but it's not just that because as the echolocation pours out of me even as we two are joined, you can see what I see. I can show you, take you down these pathways as if they are my veins. Information rolls beneath our closed eyes. Sightless, but not; we can see the ruined land beyond the tent, the bodies, the fighting that continues just beyond the debris field of the crashed ship. We can watch as alien body pierces human; you thrust into me hard, roll me over on the cot, and everything vanishes in a dark-water flood. You scream into my mouth and there is no word for the taste of you when you realize what they made of me. They took this not-human body and made it something more not-human. But ever yours as you fingerprint me, deeper, pithing.

They determine the ship is empty, but send me to its crater-lip to confirm. I scan the way the Nessik have taught me to scan. There are only dead here, on the plain and within the depth of the ship. Dead and more dead. Dead and almost dead. Nothing here is alive, save for us, you and me, and I could tell them this, but they would never believe they are already dead. They on their mountain cannot see that they are in the valley, that they will be consumed.

The division plans to move out. We pack our gear, because we go where they tell us to go; it doesn't matter what happened in the depth of that ship. It matters that we came out. We, I, me, whatever. I cannot speak the words—that I do not wish to go—but you know this as though it is your own thought as the ships lift us into the sky. We run north through the low clouds, tracing the line of destruction the aliens have left. There is one break in their path, the swath of ocean that stretches between Puerto Rico and the Dominican Republic. When the land resumes, so does their path of gluttony; we can see troops engaging them on the ground. I can feel the troops being eaten, can feel the way those muscles work to envelope, swallow, devour.

There is no accord. The press is, however, awash in such opinions—the Earth embarks upon a brand new day! Fortune favors both races! Hope was born from destruction and war!

In the trenches, we know the truth. There is no hope and no one is favored. I can speak to the Nessik and sometimes the Nessik reply, but mostly they are as angry as we are, and common ground does nothing to remedy the war. Has it ever? They hate this, we hate this, and yet, they will eat us if given the opportunity because for so long they were starving and this is all they know—swallowing a thing before they are swallowed. We do not wish to be eaten because for so long *life* is all we have known, and so.

Impasse.

Surely there is *something*, my commanders press me. I tell them of the alien war, the shipboard captivity, the eating, every mouth so impossibly hungry. But this changes nothing. Aliens, they say to explain it away; we cannot understand them, and though I *can*, I tell my commanders there is nothing. Nothing they will hear.

When I am deemed uncooperative, they try to make more of me, try to splice this ability into other soldiers, and under your hands, they do so. You spread this ability into other chimera like me in an effort for soldiers to understand the alien. Does anyone? Ever?

With a hundred thousand soldiers modified, surely there will come an answer. A pleasing answer. There does not. No matter where we travel, there is no answer that pleases. No matter the connection between you and me and the Nessik, they remain slippery, elusive—*alien*.

The Nessik will not conform, will not be remade to fit this world they crashed upon, and in the dark, when we two move as one, this delights us as it should not. Our own kind will not listen—they deserve the flood if they would not heed the warning. I reach ever out, streaming echolocation into the black where only drone eyes can see. In the dark, the Nessik endure. Thrive. They will not be eaten as they eat.

Surely there is *something*, officials press me. I was the first, surely there was a reason. A thread of logic they can follow to get out of this nightmare labyrinth.

And you press me, deeper, deeper, pithing into me.

We can feel the hive move.

Slippery, elusive, alien.

ABOUT THE AUTHOR

E. Catherine Tobler is a Sturgeon Award finalist and editor at *Shimmer Magazine*.

A Rich, Full Week
K.J. PARKER

He looked at me the way they all do. "You're him, then."

"Yes," I said.

"This way."

Across the square. A cart, tied up to a hitching-post. One thin horse. Not so very long ago, he'd used the cart for shifting dung. I sat next to him, my bag on my knees, tucking my feet in close, and laid a bet with myself as to what he'd say next.

"You don't look like a wizard," he said.

I owed myself two nomismata. "I'm not a wizard," I said.

I always say that.

"But we sent to the Fathers for a—"

"I'm not a wizard," I repeated, "I'm a philosopher. There's no such thing as wizards."

He frowned. "We sent to the Fathers for a wizard," he said.

I have this little speech. I can say it with my eyes shut, or thinking about something else. It comes out better if I'm not thinking about what I'm saying. I tell them, we're not wizards, we don't do magic, there's no such thing as magic. Rather, we're students of natural philosophy, specializing in mental energies, telepathy, telekinesis, indirect vision. Not magic; just science where we haven't quite figured out how it works yet. I looked at him. His hood and coat were homespun, that open, rather scratchy weave you get with moorland wool. The patches were a slightly different color; I guessed they'd been salvaged from an even older coat that had finally reached the point where there was nothing left to sew onto. The boots had a military look. There had been battles in these parts, thirty years ago, in the civil war. The boots looked to be about that sort of vintage. Waste not, want not.

"I'm kidding," I said. "I'm a wizard."

He looked at me, then back at the road. I hadn't risen in his estimation, but I hadn't sunk any lower, probably because that wasn't possible. I waited for him to broach the subject.

By my estimation, three miles out of town; I said; "So, tell me what's been happening."

He had big hands; too big for his wrists, which looked like bones painted color "The Brother wrote you a letter," he said.

"Yes," I replied brightly. "But I want you to tell me."

The silence that followed was thought rather than rudeness or sulking. Then he said, "No good asking me. I don't know about that stuff."

They never want to talk to me. I have to conclude that it's my fault. I've tried all sorts of different approaches. I've tried being friendly, which gets you nowhere. I've tried keeping my face shut until someone volunteers information, which gets you peace and quiet. I've read books about agriculture, so I can talk intelligently about the state of the crops, milk yields, prices at market and the weather. When I do that, of course, I end up talking to myself. Actually, I have no problem about talking to myself. In the country, it's the only way I ever get an intelligent conversation.

"The dead man," I prompted him. I never say *the deceased*.

He shrugged. "Died about three months ago. Never had any bother till just after lambing."

"I see. And then?"

"It was sheep to begin with," he said. "The old ram, with its neck broke, and then four ewes. They all reckoned it was wolves, but I said to them, wolves don't break necks, it was something with hands did that."

I nodded. I knew all this. "And then?"

"More sheep," he said, "and the dog, and then an old man, used to go round all the farms selling stuff, buttons and needles and things he made out of old bones; and when we found him, we reckoned we'd best tell the boss up at the grange, and he sent down two of his men to look out at night, and then the same thing happened to them. I said, that's no wolf. Knew all along, see. Seen it before."

That hadn't been in the letter. "Is that right?" I said.

"When I was a kid," the man said (and now I knew the problem would be getting him to shut up.) "Same thing exactly; sheep, then travelers, then three of the duke's men. My granddad, he knew what it was, but they wouldn't listen. He knew a lot of stuff, granddad."

"What happened?" I asked.

"Him and me and my cousin from out over, we got a couple of shovels and a pick and an axe, and we went and dug up this old boy who'd died. And he was all swelled up, like he'd got the gout all over, and he was *purple,* like a grape. So we cut off his head and shoveled all the dirt back, and we dropped the head down an old well, and that was the end of that. No more bother. Didn't say what we'd done, mind. The Brother wouldn't have liked it. Funny bugger, he was."

Well, I thought. "You did the right thing," he said. "Your grandfather was a clever man, obviously."

"That's right," he said. "He knew a lot of stuff."

I was doing my mental arithmetic. *When I was a kid*; so, anything from fifty-five to sixty years ago. Rather a long interval, but not unheard of. I was about to ask if anything like it had happened before then, but I figured it out just in time. If wise old Grandfather had known exactly what to do, it stood to reason he'd learned it the old-fashioned way, watching or helping; quite possibly more than once.

"The man who died," I said.

"Him." A cartload of significance crammed into that word. "Offcomer," he explained.

"Ah," I said.

"Schoolteacher, he called himself," he went on. "Dunno about that. Him and the Brother, they tried to get a school going, to teach the boys their letters and figuring and all, but I told them, waste of time in these parts, you can't spare a boy in summer, and winter, it's too dark and cold to be walking five miles there and five miles back, just to learn stuff out of a book. And they wanted paying, two pence twice a year. People round here can't afford that for a parcel of old nonsense."

I thought of my own childhood, and said nothing. "Where did he come from?"

"Down south." Well, of course he did. "I said to him, you're a long way from home. He didn't deny it. Said it was his calling, whatever that's supposed to mean."

It was dark by the time we reached the farm. It was exactly what I'd been expecting; long and low, with turf eaves a foot off the ground, turf walls over a light timber frame. No trees this high up, so lumber had to come up the coast on a big shallow-draught freighter as far as Holy Trinity, then road haulage the rest of the way. I spent the first fifteen years of my life sleeping under turf, and I still get nightmares.

Mercifully, the Brother was there waiting for me. He was younger than I'd anticipated—you always think of village Brothers as craggy old fat men, or thin and brittle, like dried twigs with papery bark. Brother Stauracius couldn't have been much over thirty; a tall, broad-shouldered man with an almost perfectly square head, hair cropped short like winter pasture and pale blue eyes. Even without the habit, nobody could have taken him for a farmer.

"I'm so glad you could come," he said, town voice, educated, rather high for such a big man. He sounded like he meant it. "Such a very long way. I hope the journey wasn't too dreadful."

I wondered what he'd done wrong, to have ended up here. "Thank you for your letter," I said.

He nodded, genuinely pleased. "I was worried, I didn't know what to put in and leave out. I'm afraid I've had no experience with this sort of thing, none at all. I'm sure there must be a great deal more you need to know."

I shook my head. "It sounds like a textbook case," I said.

"Really." He nodded several times, quickly. "I looked it up in *Statutes and Procedures*, naturally, but the information was very sparse, very sparse indeed. Well, of course. Obviously, this sort of thing has to be left to the experts. Further detail would only encourage the ignorant to meddle."

I thought about Grandfather; two shovels and an axe, job done. But not quite, or else I wouldn't be here. "Quite," I said. "Now, you're sure there were no other deaths within six months of the first attack."

"Quite sure," he said, as though his life depended on it. "Nobody but poor Anthemius."

Nobody had asked me to sit down, let alone take my wet boots off. The hell with it. I sat down on the end of a bench. "You didn't say what he died of."

"Exposure." Brother Stauracius looked very sad. "He was caught out in a snowstorm and froze to death, poor man."

"Near here?"

"Actually, no." A slight frown, like a crack in a wall. "We found him about two miles from here, as it happens, on the big pasture between the mountains and the river. A long way from anywhere, so presumably he lost his way in the snow and wandered about aimlessly until the cold got to him."

I thought about that. "On his way back home, then."

"I suppose so, yes."

I needed a map. You almost always need a map, and there never is one. If ever I'm Emperor, I'll have the entire country surveyed and mapped, and copies of each parish hung up in the temple vestries. "I don't suppose it matters," I lied. "You'll take me to see the grave."

A faint glow of alarm in those watered-down eyes. "In the morning."

"Of course in the morning," I said.

He relaxed just a little. "You'll stay here tonight, of course. I'm afraid the arrangements are a bit—"

"I was brought up on a farm," I said.

Unlike him. "That's all right, then," he said. "Now I suppose we should join our hosts. The evening meal is served rather early in these parts."

"Good," I said.

Sleeping under turf is like being in your grave. Of course, there's rafters. That's what you see when you look up, lying wide awake in the dark. Your eyes get the hang of it quite soon, diluting the black into gray into a palette of pale grays; you see rafters, not the underside of turf. And the smoke hardens it off, so it doesn't crumble. You don't get worms dropping on your face. But it's unavoidable, no matter how long you do it, no matter how used you are to it. You lie there, and the thought crosses your mind as you stare at the underside of grass; is this what it'll be like?

The answer is, of course, no. First, the roof will be considerably lower; it'll be the lid of a box, if you're lucky enough to have one, or else no roof at all, just dirt chucked on your face. Second, you won't be able to see it because you'll be dead.

But you can't help wondering. For a start, there's temperature. Turf is a wonderful insulator; keeps out the cold in winter and the heat in summer. What it doesn't keep out is the damp. It occurs to you as you lie on your back there; so long as they bury me in a thick shirt, won't have to worry about being cold, or too hot in summer, but the damp could be a problem. Gets into your bones. A man could catch his death.

It's while you're lying there—everybody else is fast asleep; no imagination, no curiosity, or they've been working so hard all day they just sleep, no matter what—that you start hearing the noises. Actually, turf's pretty quiet. Doesn't creak like wood, gradually settling, and you don't get drips from leaks. What you get is the thumping noises over your head. Clump, clump, clump, then a pause, then clump, clump, clump.

They tell you, when you're a kid and you ask, that it's the sound of dead men riding the roof-tree. They tell you that dead men get up out of the ground, climb up on the roof, sit astride the peak and jiggle about, walloping their heels into the turf like a man kicking on a horse. You believe them; I never was quite sure whether they believed it themselves. When you're older, of course, and you've left the farm and gone somewhere civilized, where it doesn't happen, you finally figure it out; what you hear is sheep, hopping up onto the roof in the night, wandering about grazing the fine sweet grass that grows there, picking out the wild leeks, of which they're particularly fond. Sheep, for crying out loud, not dead men at all. I guess they knew really, all along, and the stuff about dead men was to keep you indoors at night, keep you from wandering out under the stars (though why you should want to I couldn't begin to imagine). Or at least, at some point, way back in the dim past, some smartarse with a particularly warped imagination made up the story about dead men, to scare his kids; and the kids believed, and never figured it was sheep, and they told their kids, and so on down the generations. Maybe you never figure it out unless you leave the farm, which nobody ever does, except me.

As a matter of fact, I was just beginning to drift off into a doze when the thumping started. Clump, clump, clump; pause; clump, clump, clump. I was not amused. I was bone tired and I really wanted to get some sleep, and here were these fucking sheep walking about over my head. The hell with that, I thought, and got up.

I opened the door as quietly as I could, not wanting to wake up the household, and I stood in the doorway for a little while, letting my eyes get used to the dark. Someone had left a stick leaning against the doorframe. I picked it up, on the off chance that there might be a sheep close enough to hit.

Something was moving about again. I walked away from the house until I could see up top.

It wasn't sheep. It was a dead man.

He was sitting astride the roof, his legs drooping down either side, like a farmer on his way back from market. His hands were on his hips and he was looking away to the east. He was just a dark shape against the sky, but there was something about the way he sat there; peaceful. I didn't think he'd seen me, and I felt no great inclination to advertise my presence. If I say I wasn't scared, I wouldn't expect to be believed: but fear wasn't uppermost in my mind. Mostly, I was *interested*.

No idea how long I stood and he sat. It occurred to me that I was just assuming he was a dead man. Looked at logically, far more likely that he was alive, and had reasons of his own for climbing up on a roof in the middle of the night. Well; there's a time and a place for logic.

He turned his head, looking down the line of the roof-tree, and lifted his heels, and dug them into the turf three times; clump, clump, clump. (And at that point, I realized the flaw in my earlier rationalization. Three clumps; always three, ever since I was a kid. How many three-legged sheep do you see?) At that moment, the moon came out from behind the clouds, and suddenly we were looking at each other; me and him.

My host had been right; he was purple, like a grape. Or a bruise; the whole body one enormous bruise. Swollen, he'd said; either that, or he was an enormous man, arms and legs twice as thick as normal. His eyes were white; no pupils.

"Hello," I said.

He leaned forward just a little and cupped his hand behind his left ear. "You'll have to speak up," he said.

Words from a dead man; a purple, swollen man sitting astride a roof. "Tell me," I said, raising my voice. "Why do you do that?"

He looked at me, or a little bit past me. I couldn't tell if his mouth moved, but there was a deep, gurgling noise which could only have been laughter. "Do what?"

"Ride on the roof like it's a horse," I said.

His shoulders lifted; a slow, exaggerated shrug, like he didn't know what a shrug was, but was copying one he'd seen many years ago. "I'm not sure," he said. "I feel the urge to do it, so I do it."

Well, I thought. One of the great abiding mysteries of my childhood not quite cleared up. "Are you Anthemius?" I asked. "The schoolmaster?"

Again the laugh. "That's a very good question," he said. "Tell you what," he went on, "come up here and sit with me, so we can talk without yelling."

In the moonlight I could make out the huge hands, with their monstrous overripe fingers. How tight the skin would have to be, with all that pressure against it from the inside. Breaking a neck would be like snapping a pear off a tree.

"Let me rephrase that," I said. "Were you Anthemius? When you were—"

"Yes," he said, speaking quickly to cut off a word he didn't want to hear. "I think I was. Thank you," he added. "I've been trying to remember. It's been on the tip of my tongue, but somehow I can't seem to think of any names."

The approved procedure for coping with the restless dead is, essentially, what Grandfather did; though of course we make rather more of a fuss about it. The approved procedure should, of course, be carried out in daylight; noon is recommended. Should you chance to encounter a specimen during the night, there are two courses of action, both recommended rather than approved. One, you draw your sword and cut its head off. Two, you challenge it to the riddle-game and keep it talking all night, until dawn comes up unexpectedly and strands it like a beached whale in the cruel light.

Commentary on that. I am not a man of action. I don't vault onto roofs, I don't carry weapons. One of the reasons I left the farm in the first place was, I have trouble lifting even moderate loads. So much for option one; and as for option two—

Also, I was curious. Interested.

"What happened to you?" I said.

"You know, I'm really not sure," he replied; and the voice was starting to sound like a man's voice, my ears were getting the hang of it, the way my eyes had got used to the dark. "I know I was out in the snow and I'd lost my way. I got terribly cold, so that every bit of me hurt. Then the pain started to ease up, and I sort of fell asleep."

"You died," I said.

He didn't like me saying that, but I guess he forgave me. "I remember waking up," he said, "and it was pitch dark and terribly quiet, and I couldn't move. I was very scared. And then it occurred to me, I wasn't breathing. I don't mean I was holding my breath. I wasn't breathing at all, and it didn't matter. So then I knew."

I waited; but I hadn't got all night. "And then?"

He turned his head away. No hair, just a bulging purple scalp. A head like a plum. "I was terrified," he said. "I mean, I had no way of knowing." He paused, and I have no idea what was passing through his mind. "After a long time, I found I could move after all. I got my hands up against the lid, and I pushed, and I could feel the wood burst apart. That scared me even more, I thought the roof, I mean all the earth on top of me, I thought it'd cave in and bury me." He paused again. "I was always frightened of tight places," he said. "You know."

I nodded. Me too, as it happens.

"I guess I panicked," he went on, "because I kept pushing, and I somehow knew that I was incredibly strong, much stronger than I'd ever been before, so I thought, if I push hard enough. I wasn't thinking straight, of course."

"And then?" I asked.

"Pushed right up through the dirt and into the moonlight," he said. "Amazing feeling. The first thing I wanted to do was run to the nearest farm and tell them, Look, I'm not dead after all." He stopped; he'd said the word without thinking. "But then I thought about it; and I still wasn't breathing, and I couldn't actually *feel* anything. I could move my hands and feet, I could stand upright and balance, all that, but—you know when you've been sitting a long time and your feet go numb. It was like that, all over. It felt so strange."

"Go on," I said.

He didn't, not for a long time. "I think I sat down," he said. "I don't know why I'd have done that, standing up didn't make me tired or anything. I don't feel tired, ever. But I was so confused, I didn't know what I was supposed to do. It all felt wrong." He lifted his heels slowly and let them drop; clump, clump, clump. "And while I was there the sun started to come up, and the light just sort of flooded into my head and bleached everything away, so I couldn't think at all. I guess you could say I passed out. Anyway, when I opened my eyes I was back where I'd started from, lying in the dark."

I frowned. "How did you get back there?"

"I just don't know," he said. "Still don't. It always happens, that's all I know. When the sun comes up, my mind washes away. If I've gone any distance, I know I have to get back. I run. I can run really fast. I know I've got to be back—home," he said, with a sort of breaking-up laugh, "before the sun comes up. I've learned to be careful, to give myself plenty of time."

He was still and quiet for a while. I asked, "Why do you kill things?"

"No idea." He sounded distressed. "If something comes close enough, I grab it and twist it till it's dead. Like a cat lashing out at a bit of string. Reflex. I just know it's something I have to do."

I nodded. "Do you go looking—?"

"Yes." He mumbled the word, like a kid admitting a crime. "Yes, I do. I do my best to keep away from where there might be people. It's all the same to me; sheep, foxes, men. I'd go a long way away, into the mountains, if I could. But I have to stay close, so I can get back in time."

I'd been debating with myself, and I knew I had to ask. "What were you?" I said. "What did you do?"

He didn't answer. I repeated the question.

"Like you said," he replied. "I was a schoolteacher."

"Before that."

When he answered, it was against his will. The words came out slow, flat; he spoke because he had to. "I was a Brother," he said. "When I was thirty, they said I should apply to the Order, they thought I had the gift, and the brains, and the application and the self-discipline. I passed the exam and I was at the Studium for five years. Like you," he added.

I let that go. "You joined the Order."

"No." The flat voice had gone; there was a flare of anger. "No, I failed matriculation. I retook it the next year, but I failed again. They sent me back to my parish, but by then they'd got someone else. So I ended up wandering about, looking for teaching work, letter-writing, anything I could do to earn a living. There's not a lot you can do, of course."

Suddenly I felt bitter cold, right through. Took me a moment to realize it was fear. "So you came here," I said, just to keep him talking.

"Eventually. A lot of other places first, but here's where I ended up." He lifted his head abruptly. "They sent you here to deal with me, am I right?"

I didn't reply.

"Of course they did," he said. "Of course. I'm a nuisance, a pest, a menace to agriculture. You came here to dig me up and cut my head off."

This time, I was the one who had to speak against my will. "Yes."

"Of course," he said. "But I can't let you do that. It's my—"

He'd been about to say life. Presumably he tried to find another way of phrasing it, then gave up. We both knew what he meant.

"You passed the exams, then," he said.

"Barely," I replied. "Two hundred seventh out of two hundred twenty."

"Which is why you're here."

His white eyes in the ash-white moonlight. "That's right," I said. "They don't give out research posts if you come two hundred seventh."

He nodded gravely. "Commercial work," he said.

"When I can get it," I replied. "Which isn't often. Others far more qualified than me."

He grunted. It could have been sympathy. "Public service work."

"Afraid so," I replied.

"Which is why you're here." He lifted his head and rolled it round on his shoulders, like someone waking up after sleeping in a chair. "Because—well, because you aren't much good. Well?"

I resented that, even though it was true. "It's not that I'm not good," I said. "It's just that everyone in my year was better than me."

"Of course." He leaned forward, his hands braced on his knees. "The question is," he said, "do I still have the gift, after what happened to me. If I've still got it, your job is going to be difficult."

"If not," I said.

"Well," he replied, "I suppose we're about to find out."

"Indeed," I said. "There could be a paper for the journals in this."

"Your chance to escape from obscurity," he said solemnly. "Under different circumstances, I'd wish you well. Unfortunately, I really don't want you cutting off my head. It's a miserable existence, but—"

I could see his point. His voice was quite human now; if I'd known him before, I'd have recognized him. He had his back to the moon, so I couldn't see the features of his face.

"What I'm trying to say is, you don't have to do it," he said. "Go away. Go home. Nobody knows you came out here tonight. I promise I'll stay away until you've gone. If I don't show up, you can report that there was no direct evidence of an infestation, and therefore you didn't feel justified in desecrating what was probably an innocent grave."

"But you'll be back," I said.

"Yes, and no doubt they'll send someone else," he said. "But it won't be you."

I was tempted. Of course I was tempted. For one thing, he was a rational creature; with my eyes shut, if I hadn't known better, I'd have said he was a natural man with a heavy cold. And what if the gift did survive death? He'd kill me. I had to admit it to myself; the thought that I could get killed doing this job hadn't occurred to me. I'd anticipated a quick, grisly hour's work in broad daylight; no risk.

I'm not a coward, but I appreciate the value of fear, the way I appreciate the value of money. I'm most definitely not brave.

I saw something in the moonlight, and said (trying not to talk quickly or raise my voice); "I could go back to bed, and then come back in the morning and dig you up."

"You could," he said.

"You don't think I would."

"Not if we'd made an agreement."

"You could be right," I said. "But what about the farmers? You've got to admit—"

At which moment, the Brother (who'd come out of the back door, crawled up on the roof behind him and edged down the roof-tree towards him until he was close enough to reach his neck with the axe he'd brought with him) raised his arms high and swung. No sound at all; but at the last moment, the dead man leaned his head to one side, just enough, and the axe blade swept past, cutting air. I heard the Brother grunt, shocked and panicky; I saw the dead man—eyes still fixed on me—reach behind him with his left hand and catch the swinging axe just below the head, and hold it perfectly still. The Brother gasped, but didn't let go; he was pulling with all his strength, like a little dog tugging on a belt. All his efforts couldn't move the dead man's arm the thickness of a fingernail.

"Now," the dead man said. "Let's see."

The delay on my part was unforgivable, completely unprofessional. I knew I had to do something, but my mind had gone completely blank. I couldn't remember any procedures, let alone any words. *Think,* a tiny voice was yelling inside me head, but I couldn't. I heard the Brother whimper, as he applied every scrap of strength in a tendon-ripping, joint-tearing last desperate jerk on the axe handle that had no effect whatsoever. The dead man was looking straight at me. His lips began to move.

Pro nobis peccatoribus; not the obvious choice, not even on the same page of the book, but it was the only procedure I could think of.

Unfortunately, it's one I've always had real difficulties with. You reach out with your hand that is not a hand, extend the fingers that aren't fingers; I'm all right as far as that, and then I tend to come unstuck.

(What I was thinking was: So he failed the exam, and I passed. Yes, but maybe the reason he failed was, he didn't read the questions through properly, or he spent so long on Part 1 that he didn't leave himself enough time for two and three. Maybe he's really good, just unlucky in exams.)

I was mumbling; *Sol invicte, ora pro nobis peccatoribus in die periculi.* Of course, there's a school of thought that says the magic words have no real effect whatsoever, they're just a way of concentrating the mind. I tend to agree. Why should an archaic prayer in a dead language to a god nobody's believed in for six hundred years have any effect on anything at all? *Ora pro nobis peccatoribus,* I repeated urgently, *nobis peccatoribus in die periculi.*

It worked, It can't have been the words, of course, but it felt like it was the words. I was in, I was through. I was inside his head.

There was nothing there.

Believe me, it's true. Nothing at all; like walking into a house where someone's died, and the family have been in and cleared out all the furniture. Nothing there, because I was inside the head of a dead man; albeit a dead man who was looking at me reproachfully out of blank white eyes while holding an axe absolutely still.

Fine; all the easier, if it's empty. I looked for the controls. You have to visualize them, of course. I see them as the handwheels of a lathe. It's because I had a holiday job in a foundry in Second Year. I don't know how to use a lathe. What I mostly did was sweep up piles of swarf off the floor.

Here is the handwheel that controls the arms. I reached out with the hand that is not a hand, grabbed it and tried to turn it. Stuck. I tried harder. Stuck. I tried really hard, and the bloody thing came away in my hand.

It's not supposed to do that.

I re-visualized. I saw the controls as the reins of a cart, the footbrake under my boot that was not a boot. I stamped on the brake and hauled back hard on the reins.

I haven't got round to writing that paper for the journals, so here it is for the first time anywhere. The gift does not survive death. Nothing survives. The room was empty. And the handwheel only broke off because I'm clumsy and cack-handed, the sort of person who trips over cats and breaks the nibs of pens by pressing too hard.

I heard the Brother gasp, as he jerked the axe out of the dead man's grip. The dead man didn't move. His eyes were still fixed on mine, right up to the moment when the axe shore through his neck and his head wobbled and fell, bounced off his knee and tumbled off the roof into the short grass below. The body didn't move.

I know why. It took ten of us, with an improvised crane made of twelve-foot three-inch fir poles, to get the body down off the roof. It must've weighed half a ton. The head alone was two hundredweight. Two men couldn't lift it; they had to use levers to roll it along the ground. There was no blood, but the neck started to ooze a milky white juice that smelt worse than anything you could possibly imagine.

We burned the body. We drenched it in pine-pitch, and it caught quite easily and burnt down to nothing; not even any recognizable bits of bone. The white juice flared up like oil. They rolled the head over to the slurry-pond and pitched it in. It went down with a gurgle and a burp.

"I heard you talking to it," the Brother told me. For some reason, the word *it* offended me. "I guessed you were using a variation on the riddle game, to keep it distracted till the sun came up."

"Something like that," I said.

He nodded. "I shouldn't have interfered, I'm sorry," he said. "You had the situation under control, and I could have ruined everything."

"That's all right," I said.

He smiled; as if to say, it wasn't all right, but thanks for forgiving me. "I guess I panicked," he said. Then he frowned. "No, I didn't. I saw a chance of getting in on the act. It was stupid and selfish of me. You'll have to write to the prebendary."

"I don't see why," I said mildly. "The way I see it, your actions were open to several different interpretations. I choose to interpret them as courage and resourcefulness. I could put that in a letter, if you like."

"Would you?" In his face, I saw all the desperation and cruelty of sudden, unexpected hope. "I mean, seriously?"

"Of course," I said.

"That'd be—" He stopped. He couldn't think of a big enough word. "You've got no idea what it's like," he said; all in a rush, like diarrhea. "Being stuck here, in this miserable place with these appalling people. If I can't get back to a town, I swear I'll go mad. And it's so cold in winter. I hate the cold."

You can sleep in the coach, Father Prior said, when I tried to make a fuss about the timetable. I didn't say to him; have you ever been on a provincial mailcoach, on country roads, at this time of year? A dead man couldn't sleep on a mailcoach.

I slept, nearly all the way; on account, I guess, of not having had much sleep the night before. Woke up just as we were crossing the Fulvens bridge; I looked out of the window, and all I could see was water, moonlight reflected on water. Couldn't get back to sleep after that. Too dark to read the case notes, which I'd neglected to do back at the farm. But I remembered the basic facts from the briefing. These jobs are all the same, anyhow. Piece of cake.

The coach threw me out just after dawn, at a crossroads in the middle of nowhere. Somewhere up on the moors; I'm a valley boy myself. We had cousins up on the moor. I hated it when they came to visit. The old man was deaf as a post, and the three boys (mid to late thirties, but they were always the boys) just sat there, not saying a word. The mother died young, and I can't say I blame her.

They were supposed to be meeting the coach, but there was no one there. I stood for a while, then I sat on my bag, then I sat on the ground, which was damp. I heard an owl, and a fox, or at least I hope it was a fox. If not, it was something we never got around to covering in Third Year, and I'm very glad I didn't see it.

They arrived eventually, in a little dog-cart thing; an old man driving, a younger man and the Brother. One small pony, furry like a bear.

The Brother did the talking, for which I was quite grateful. He was one of the better sort of country Brothers; short man, somewhere between fifty and sixty, a distinct burr to his voice but he spoke clearly and used proper words. The boy was the younger man's son, the older man's grandson. He'd been fooling about in a big oak tree, slipped, fell; broken arm and a hideous bash on the head. He hadn't come round, and it had been a week now. They had to prise his mouth open with the back of a horn spoon to get food and water in; he swallowed all right, but that was all he did. You could stick a needle in his foot half an inch and he wouldn't even twitch. The swelling on the back of his head had gone down—the Brother disclaimed any medical knowledge, but he was lying—and they'd set the arm and splinted it, for what that was worth.

I thought; better than killing the restless dead. One of my best subjects at the Studium, though of course we did all our practicals on conscious minds, with a Father sitting a few feet away, watching like a hawk. I'd done one about eighteen months earlier, and it went off just fine; in, found her, straight out again. She followed me like a dog. I'd been relieved when Father Prior told me; it could've been something awkward and fiddly, like auspices, or horrible and scary, like a possession. Just in case, I'd brought the book. I'd meant to mug up the relevant chapter, either at the farm or on the coach, but I hadn't got round to it. Anyway, it had to be better than that empty place.

It was quite a big house, for a hill-farm; sitting in the well of a valley, with a dense copper-beech hedge on all four sides, as a windbreak. Just the five of them in the house, the Brother said; grandfather, father, mother, the boy and a hired man who slept in the hayloft. The boy was nine years old. The Brother told me his name, but I'm hopeless with names.

They asked me, did I want to rest after the journey; wash and brush up, something to eat? The correct answer was, of course, No, so I gave it.

"He's in here," the Brother said.

Big for a hill-farm, but still oppressively small. Downstairs, the big kitchen, with a huge table, fireplace, two hams swinging like dead men on gibbets. A parlor, tiny and dusty and cold. Dairy, scullery, store; doorway through to the cowstalls. Upstairs, one big room and a sort of oversized cupboard, where the boy was. I could just about kneel beside the bed, if I didn't mind the window-sill digging in the small of my back.

The hell with that, I thought; I'm a qualified man, a professional, a Father; a wizard. I shouldn't have to work in conditions you wouldn't keep pigs in. "Take him downstairs," I said. "Put him on the kitchen table."

They had a job. The stairs in that house were like a bell-tower, tightly coiled and cramped. Father and grandfather did the heavy lifting, while I watched. It's an odd thing about me. Sometimes, the more compassion is called for, the less capable I am of feeling it. I offer no explanation or excuse.

"He shouldn't have been moved," the Brother hissed in my ear, just loud enough so that everyone could hear. "In his condition—"

"Yes, thank you," I said, in my best arrogant-city-bastard voice. I couldn't say why I was behaving like this. Sometimes I do. "Now, if you'll all stay well back, I'll see what I can do."

I looked at the boy, and I could remember the theory perfectly, every last detail, every last lecture note. His eyes were closed; he had a stupid face, fat girly lips, fat cheeks. If he lived, he'd grow up tall, solid, double-chinned, gormless; the son of the farm. Pork fat and home-brewed beer; he'd be spherical by the time he was forty, strong enough to wrestle a bullock to its knees, slow and tireless, infuriatingly calm, a man of few words; respected at market, shrewd and fat, his bald patch hidden under a hat that would never come off, probably not even in bed. A solid, productive life, which it was my duty to save. Lucky me.

Theory; theory is your lifeline, they used to tell me, your driftwood in a shipwreck. I reminded myself of the basic propositions.

To recover a lost mind, first make an entrance. This is usually done by visualizing yourself as a penetrating object; a drill bit, a woodpecker's beak, a maggot. The drill bit works for me, though for some reason I tend to be a carpenter's auger, wound in with a brace. I go in through the spiral flakes of waste bone thrown clear by the wide grooves of the cutter. I assume it's from some childhood memory, watching Granddad at work in the barn. You're not really supposed to use personal memories, but it's easier, for someone with my limited imagination.

Once you're in; first ward, immediately, because you never know what might be waiting for you in there. I raised first ward as soon as I felt myself go through. I use *scutum fidei,* visualize a shield. Mine's round, with a hole in it at twelve o'clock so I can see what's going on.

I peered through the hole. No nasty creatures with dripping fangs crouched to pounce, which was nice. Count to ten and lower the shield slowly.

I looked around. This is the crucial bit, and you mustn't rush. How long it takes depends on the strength of your gift, so naturally I take ages. The light gradually increases. First things first; get your bearings. Orientate yourself, taking special care to get a fix on the point you came in by. Well, obviously. If you lose your entry-point, you're stuck; in someone else's head forever. You really don't want that.

I lined up on the corners of a ceiling, drawing diagonal lines and fixing on their point of origin, measuring the angles with my imaginary protractor (it's brass, with numbers in gothic-italic) One-oh-five, seventy-five; repeat the numbers four times out loud, to make sure they're loaded into memory. Fine. Now I know where I am and how to get out again. One-oh-five, seventy-five. Now, then. Let the dog see the rabbit.

I was in a room. It's nearly always an interior; with kids, practically guaranteed it's their bedroom, or the room they sleep in, depending on social class and domestic arrangements. In all relevant essentials, it was the room upstairs I had him carried down from. Excellent; nice and small, not many places to hide anything. So much easier when you're dealing with a subject of limited intelligence.

I visualized a body for myself. I tend not to be me. With children, it's usually best to be a nice lady; the kid's mother, if possible. I'm not good enough to do specific people, and I have real problems being women. So I was a nice old man instead.

Hello, I said. Where are you?

Don't worry if they don't answer. Sometimes, they do, sometimes they don't. I walked round the bed, knelt down, looked under it. There was a cupboard; one of those triangular jobs, wedged in a corner. I opened that. For some reason, it was full of the skins and bones of dead animals. None of my business; I closed it. I pulled the covers off the bed, and lifted the pillow.

Odd, I thought, and touched base with theory. The boy must still be alive, or else there would be no room. If he's alive, he must be in here somewhere. He can't be invisible, not inside his own head. He can, of course, be anything he likes, so long as it's animate and alive. A cockroach, for example, or a flea. I sighed. I get all the rotten jobs.

I adjusted the scale, making the room five times bigger. Go up in easy stages. If he was being a cockroach, he'd now be a rat-sized cockroach. If he was being a rat, of course, he'd be cat-sized and capable of giving me a nasty bite. I used *lorica*, just in case. I looked under the bed again.

I visualized a clock, in the middle of the wall opposite the door. It told me I'd been inside for ten minutes. The recommended maximum is thirty. Really first-rate practitioners have been known to stay in for an hour and still come out more or less in one piece; that's material for a leading article in the journals. I searched again, this time paying more attention to the contents of the cupboard. Dried, desiccated animal skins; squirrels, rabbits, rats. No fleas, mites or ticks. So much for that theory.

I visualized a glass jug, to represent my energy level. You can use yourself up surprisingly quickly and not know it. Just as well I did. My jug was a third empty. You want to save at least a fifth just to get out again. I visualized calibrations, so as to be sure.

Quick think. The recommended course of action would be to visualize a tracking agent (spaniel, terrier, ferret) but that takes a fair chunk of your resources; also, it burns energy while it's in use, and getting rid of it takes energy, too. I drew a distinct red line on my measuring-jug, and a blue line just above it. The alternative to a tracker is to increase the scale still further; twenty times, say, in which case your cockroach will be a wolf-sized monster that could jump you and bite your head off. I was still running *lorica,* but any effective ward burns energy. If I found myself with a fight on my hands, I could dip below that essential red line in a fraction of a second. No, the hell with that.

I visualized a terrier. I'm not a dog person, so my terrier was a bit odd; very short, stumpy legs and a rectangular head. Still, it went at it with great enthusiasm, wagging its imaginary tail and making little yapping noises. All round the room, nose into everything. Then it sat on the floor and looked at me, as if to say, Well?

Not looking good. My jug was half empty, I'd used up my repertoire of approved techniques, and found nothing. Just my luck to get a special case, a real collector's item. Senior research fellows would be fighting each other for the chance of a go at this one, but I just wanted to get the job done and clear out. Wasted on me, you might say.

I vanished the dog. Quick think. There had to be something else I could try, but nothing occurred to me. Didn't make sense; he had to be in here somewhere, or there'd be no room. He couldn't be invisible. He could only turn himself into something he could imagine—and it had to be real; no fantasy creatures the size of a pin-head. At five times magnification, a red mite would be plainly visible; also, the dog would've found it. Tracking agents, even inferior ones visualized by me, smell life. If he was in here, the dog would've found him.

So—

As required by procedure, I considered abandoning the attempt and getting out. This would, of course, mean the boy would die; you can't go back in twice, that's an absolute. I'd be within my rights, faced with an enigma on this scale. The failure would be noted on my record, of course, but there'd be an annotation, *no blame attaches,* and it wouldn't be the first time, not by a long way. The kid would die; not my problem. I'd have done my best, and that's all you have to do.

Or I could think of something. Such as what?

They tell you; be wise, don't improvise. If in doubt, get out. Making stuff up as you go along is mightily frowned on, in much the same way as you're not encouraged to fry eggs in a fireworks factory. There's no knowing what you might invent, and outside controlled conditions, invention could lead to the Cartographic Commission having to redraw the maps for a whole county. Or you could make a hole in a wall, which is the worst thing anybody can do. At the very least, I'd be sure to end up in front of a Board, facing charges of unauthorized innovation and divergence. Saving the life of some farm kid would be an excuse, but not a very good one.

I could think of something. Such as—

There's no such thing as magic. Instead, there's the science we don't properly understand, not yet. There are effects that work, and we have no idea why. One of these is *spes aeternitatis,* a wretchedly inconsistent, entirely inexplicable conjuring trick that no self-respecting Father would condescend to use. That's because they can't get it to work reliably.

I can.

Spes aeternitatis is an appearances-adjuster. You can use it to find hidden objects, or translate lies, or tell if a slice of cake or a glass of wine's got poison in it. I do it by visualizing everything that's wrong in light blue. It's a tiny little scrap of talent that I've got and practically everybody else hasn't; it's like being double-jointed, or wiggling your nostrils like a rabbit.

I closed my eyes and opened them again, and saw a light blue room. Everything light blue. Everything false.

Oh, I thought; then, one-oh-five, seventy five, and I started lining up diagonals for my escape. But that wasn't to be, unfortunately. The room blurred and reappeared, and it was all different. It was my room; the room I slept in until I was fifteen years old.

He was sitting on the end of the bed; a slight man, almost completely bald, with a small nose and a soft chin, small hands, short, thin legs. I'd put him at about fifty years old. His skin was purple, like a grape.

"You were wrong," he said, looking up at me. "The talent survives death."

"That's interesting," I said. "How did you get in here?"

He smiled. "You practically invited me in," he said. "When I heard that fool behind me, with the axe, I looked at you. You felt sorry for me. You thought; is he not a man and a Brother, or words to that effect. I used Stilicho's transport, and here I am."

I nodded. "I should've put up wards."

"You should. Careless. Attention to detail isn't your strongest suit."

"The boy," I said.

He shrugged. "In there somewhere, I dare say. But we aren't in his head, we're in yours. I've made myself at home, as you can see."

I looked round quickly. The apple-box with the bottom knocked out, where I used to keep my books; it was where it should be, but the books were different. They were new and beautifully bound in tooled calf, and the alphabet their titles were written in was strange to me.

"My memories," I said.

He waved his hand. "Well rid of them," he said. "Misery and failure, a life wasted, a talent dissipated. You'll be better off."

I nodded. "With yours."

"Quite. Oh, they're not pleasant reading," he said, with a scowl. "Bitter, angry; memories of bigotry and spite, relentless bad luck, a life of constant setbacks and reverses, a talent misunderstood. You'll see that I failed the exam the second time because, sitting there in Great School, I suddenly hit on a much better way of achieving *unam sanctam*; quicker, safer, ruthlessly efficient. I tried it out as soon as the exam was over, and it worked. But I got no marks, so they failed me. I ask you, where's the sense in that?"

"You failed the retake," I said. "What about the first time?"

He laughed. "I had the flu," he said. "I was practically delirious, could barely remember my name. Would they listen? No. Rules. You see what I mean. Bad luck and spite at every turn."

I nodded. "What happens to me?"

He looked at me. "You'll be better off," he repeated.

"I'll stop existing. I'll be dead."

"Not physically," he said mildly. "Your body, my mind. Your fully qualified licensed-practitioner's body, and a mind that saw how to improve *unam sanctam* in a half-second flash of intuition."

It says a lot about my self-esteem that I actually considered it, though not for very long. Half a second, maybe. "What happens now?" I asked. "Do we fight, or—?"

He shrugged."If you like," he said, and extended his arm. It was ten feet long, thick as a gatepost. He gripped my throat like a man holding a mouse, and crushed me.

I guess I was about seventy percent dead when I remembered; I know what to do. I drew a rather shaky second ward; he closed his fingers on thin air, and I was standing behind him.

He swung round, roaring like a bull. He had bull's horns sticking out of his forehead. I tried second ward again, but he got there before I did, grabbed my head and smashed my face into the wall.

Just in time, I remembered; there is no pain. I used Small Mercies, softening the wall into felt, and slipped through his fingers. I was smoke. I hung above him in a cloud. He laughed, and fetched me back with *vis mentis*. The back of my head hit the floor, which gave way like a mattress. I became a spear, and buried myself in his chest. He used second ward and was the other side of the room.

"You fight like a first-year," he said.

Which was true. I clenched my mind like a fist; the walls closed in on him, squashing him like a spider under a boot. I felt him, like a nail right through the sole. Back to first ward, and we stood glowering at each other, in opposite corners of the room.

"You can't beat me," he said. "I'll wear you down and you'll simply fade away. Face it, what the hell have you got to live for?"

Valid point. "All right, then," I said.

His eyes opened wide. "I win?"

"You win," I said.

He was pleased; very pleased. He grinned at me and raised his hand, just as I got my fingers round the handle of the door and twisted as hard as I could.

He saw that and opened his mouth to scream. But the door flew open, knocking me back. I closed my eyes. The door was, of course, the intersection of two lines drawn diagonally across the room, at 105 and 75 degrees precisely.

I opened my eyes. He'd gone. I was in the boy's room, the room upstairs. The boy was sitting on the floor, legs crossed, hands under his chin. He looked up at me.

"Well, come on," I snapped at him. "I haven't got all day."

They were pathetically grateful. Mother in floods of tears, father clinging to my arm, how can we ever thank you, it's a miracle, you're a miracle-worker. I wasn't in the mood. The boy, lying on the kitchen table under a pile of blankets, looked up at me and frowned, as though something about me wasn't quite right. A quiet, analytical stare; it bothered the hell out of me. I refused food and drink and made father get out the pony and trap and take me out to the crossroads. But the mail won't be arriving for six hours, he objected; it's cold and dark, you'll catch your death.

I didn't feel cold.

At the crossroads, huddling under the smelly old hat father insisted on giving me, I tried to search my mind, to see if he'd really gone. There was, of course, no way he could have survived. I'd opened the door (Rule One; never open the door) and he'd been sucked out of my head out into the open, where there was no talented mind to receive him. Even if he was as strong as he'd claimed to be, there was no way he could have lasted more than three seconds before he broke up and dissipated into the air. There was absolutely nothing he could have done, no way he could have survived.

The coach arrived. I got on it, and slept all the way. At the inn, I got a lamp and a mirror, and examined myself all over. Just when I thought I was all clear, I found a patch of purple skin, about the size of a crab apple, on the calf of my left leg. I told myself it was just a bruise.

(That was a year ago. It's still there.)

The rest of the round was just straightforward stuff; a possession, a small rift, a couple of incursions, which I sealed with a strong closure and duly reported when I got back. Since then, I've volunteered for a screening, been to see a couple of counselors, bought a pair of full-length mirrors. And I've been promoted; field officer, superior grade. They're quite pleased with me, and no wonder. I seem to be getting better at the job all the time. And I'm writing a paper, would you believe; modifications to *unam sanctam*. Quicker, safer, much more efficient. So blindingly obvious, I'm surprised no one's ever thought of it before.

Father Prior is surprised but pleased. I don't know what's got into you, he said.

First published in *Swords & Dark Magic: The New Sword and Sorcery,*
edited by Jonathan Strahan and Lou Anders.

ABOUT THE AUTHOR

K.J. Parker was born long ago and far away, worked as a coin dealer, a dogs-body in an auction house and a lawyer, and has so far published thirteen novels (the Fencer, Scavenger and Engineer trilogies, and standalone novels *The Company, The Folding Knife, The Hammer,* and *Sharps*), three novellas ('Purple And Black,' 'Blue And Gold' and 'A Small Price To Pay For Birdsong,' which won the 2012 World Fantasy Award) and a gaggle of short fiction. Married to a lawyer and living in the south west of England, K.J. Parker is a mediocre stockman and forester, a barely competent carpenter, blacksmith and machinist, a two-left-footed fencer, lackluster archer, utility-grade armorer, accomplished textile worker and crack shot. K.J. Parker is not K.J. Parker's real name. However, if K.J. Parker were to tell you K.J. Parker's real name, it wouldn't mean anything to you.

Wizard's Six

ALEX IRVINE

1

In the spring Paulus set out north from The Fells, hunting the apprentice Myros. He cannot be allowed to collect his six, the wizard had said. If you cannot find his track, you must kill whichever of the six he has already selected. It did Paulus' conscience no good to kill people whose only fault was being collected by an aspiring wizard, but he would be only the first of many hunters. Without the guild's protection, a wizard's six were like baby turtles struggling toward the sea. Best to spare them a life of being hunted.

The apprentice had spent enough time in the Agate Tower to know that there would be pursuit. He was moving fast and had four months' head start; Paulus moved faster, riding through nights and spring storms, fording spring-swollen rivers, asking quiet questions over bottles in public houses along the only road over the mountains. He killed the first of the apprentice's collection on a farm between a bend in the road and a ripple of foothills: a small boy with a dirty face and a stick in his hand.

Yes, mister, a man passed by here in the winter.

Yes, mister, he had a ring over his glove. I was feeding the pig, and he told me I was a likely boy. Are you looking for him?

Can I see your sword?

They weren't supposed to choose children, Paulus was thinking as he rode on. Even apart from the cultural sanction, children's magic was powerful but unpredictable, tricky to harness. No wonder the guild was after this one.

In a public house that evening, the day's chill slowly ebbing from his feet, Paulus said a prayer for the boy's parents. He hoped they hadn't sent anyone after him. It was bad enough to kill children; he had even less desire to take the lives of vengeful bumpkins. Best to keep moving. Already he had gained a month on the apprentice, who was moving fast for a normal man but not fast enough to stay ahead of Paulus, who had once been one of the king's rangers. Upstairs in his room, Paulus watched a thin drift of snow appear on the windowsill, spilling onto the plank floor. His prayer beads worked through his fingers. Go, boy, he thought. Speed your way to heaven. He dreamed of turtles, and of great birds that flew at night.

In the morning the snow had stopped, and Paulus cut a piece of cheese from a wheel left out in the kitchen. He stuck the knife in the remaining cheese and set a coin next to it, then left through the back door and saddled his horse without waking the stable boy. He rode hard, into the mountains and over the first of the passes where the road lay under drifted snow taller than a man on horseback. The horse picked out the track; like Paulus, it had been this way before. It was blowing hard by noon, when they had come to the bottom of a broad valley dotted with farms and a single manor house. Paulus rode to the gates of the manor and waited to be noticed.

The gate creaked open, revealing a choleric elder in threadbare velvet, huddled under a bearskin cloak. "Who comes to the house of Baron Branchefort?"

Paulus dismounted and let the seneschal see the sigil of the Agate Tower dangling from the horse's bridle. "I ride on an errand from the wizards' guild in The Fells," he said. "Has an apprentice traveled through this valley?"

"And how would I know an apprentice?"

"He would wear a ring over the glove on his right hand. He is called Myros."

The elder nodded. "Aye, he was here. Visited the Baron asking permission to gather plant lore."

"Was this granted?"

"It was. He was our guest for a week and a day, then rode to the head of the valley."

"Did he gather any herbs?"

"I did not observe."

"You wouldn't have. His errand has nothing to do with plants. He travels to collect children."

The elder held Paulus' gaze for a long moment. "This is why you follow him."

"It is. Are there children in your house?"

"No. The Baron nears his eightieth year. We have few servants, and no children."

Paulus offered up a prayer of thanks that he would not have to enter the manor. He had seen more than enough of noble houses fallen into somnolence. Standing at the gate of this one, his chest constricted and he thought of his brother.

"Where," he asked, "are the houses in this valley with children?"

The elder looked up at the sky, then down at the ground between his feet. "Many children come into this world," he said. "Few survive. Only one of the Baron's vassals has children below marriageable age. He is called Philo, and his house is the last before the road rises into the mountains again."

Paulus nodded and mounted his horse again.

"You will ease Philo's mind, I pray," the elder said.

"What ease I can give, I will give," Paulus said, and rode north.

Philo's house lay in the shadow of a double peak, across the saddle of which lay Paulus' route over the mountains. As Paulus rode up, the sun rested between the peaks. A man about Paulus' age, but with the caved-in chest and stooped neck of too much work and not enough food, was drawing water. A girl of seven or eight years stood waiting with an empty bucket.

"Philo," Paulus said.

"That is my name," Philo said, without looking up at Paulus, as he hauled a full bucket over the edge of the well. He emptied it into the bucket his daughter set on the ground at his feet. "And this is my daughter Sophia. Now you know what of us is worth knowing."

"A young man wearing a ring over his glove has been here," Paulus said.

Philo dropped the bucket back into the well. "He has."

"He spoke to your daughter."

"That's right, sir, he did. Told her she was a likely girl. She's always seemed so to me, but if I was any judge of men or girls I wouldn't be here." Still Philo had not met Paulus' gaze. Paulus began to wonder what had passed between him and Myros; or was his demeanor caused by the Brancheforts?

No matter.

"I come from The Fells," Paulus said. "My instructions are to gather the girl he spoke to. For service at the Agate Tower."

At this, Philo looked up and Paulus and put a hand around his daughter's thin shoulders. Now it was Paulus who wanted to look away. He forced himself to hold Philo's eye. "She's my only, sir," Philo said. "And my wife, we're too old to have another."

"Philo," Paulus said. "I have no quarrel with you. My errand is my errand."

He watched the awful calculus of the peasant on Philo's face. One fewer mouth to feed. Giving his daughter over to a life of service with the wizards of The Fells, where she would spend the rest of her days forgetting what it was like to go to bed hungry. And against that . . .

"May we visit her, sir?"

"When she has been gone a year," Paulus said. He was a poor liar, but this provision he remembered from his own journey to The Fells as a boy, when he had been taken into the King's Acrobats.

His mother had never come. After a year he had stopped expecting her.

"Before that," he said, "she will still long for home. You may write as long as you do not ask her to return. Censors at the guild will destroy your letters if you do."

Philo was nodding slowly. "We do love her, sir," he said. "She's our only."

And through all this, the girl Sophia spoke not a word.

"I will return in the morning," Paulus said.

The ruse had cost him a day, and cost him, too, any chance of a better meal than jerky eaten under a tree. Paulus had started back to the manor house, then veered away from the road into a copse of beech and spruce. He had already lied more that day than during the previous ten years, and could no more maintain his fabrications than strike down young Sophia of Branchefort Valley in her father's presence. So he hobbled his horse, found dry ground beneath the spreading branches of a spruce tree, and prayed until sleep came. Then he dreamed of his mother, refusing to look at him as he craned his neck to see through the wagon gate and cried out *Mama, goodbye, Mama.*

In the morning, Sophia was waiting in the lambskin coat Philo had been wearing the afternoon before. Rabbit fur wrapped her feet, and she held a small satchel in both hands. Philo and her mother stood behind her, each with a hand on her; the woman's hand moved to smooth the coat's collar, tug a tangle out of Sophia's hair. Philo reached down and took his daughter's hand.

"May she write us?" the woman said.

"After a year, ma'am," answered Paulus. "Should she prove unsuitable, I will bring her back myself, with no dishonor to you. It's many a child isn't meant for the wizards' service."

"Not unsuitable, not our Sophia," Philo said. He swallowed.

"Philo," Paulus said. "Can you spare this coat? She will be warm on the journey."

"I'd like her to have it," Philo said. "It's all we can give her."

Paulus could come up with no convincing reply. "There's fresh eggs and bread in the bag," Sophia's mother said.

"I thank you, ma'am," Paulus said. "I am Paulus. Your man and I met yesterday."

"I am Clio, sir," she said. She was looking hard at him—seeing, Paulus knew, the scars on his hands and the long sword on his right hip.

"Your daughter has her destiny, Clio," Paulus said. "I am here to take her to it."

Baby turtles, he told himself. Another might have killed all three by now, and moved on. The thought gave him no ease. He averted his eyes as Philo and Clio made their farewells. Braver than either, Sophia took Paulus' hand and climbed onto the saddle in front of him. A tremor ran through her small body, but she reached out to get her fists into the horse's mane. She looked back at her parents as Paulus spurred the horse northward, and he wondered what she saw.

When she spoke, much later when the northern pass out of Branchefort Valley was behind them, Paulus didn't register her voice at first. He was thinking about the boy who had been feeding his pig when Myros came. How easily children died. "Sir?" the girl said. "What do you call the horse?"

"I never named him," Paulus said.

"Can I call him Brown?"

"All right."

"Your name is Brown," Sophia told the horse.

He could kill her at any time, could have killed her at any moment since crossing the pass. Could, for that matter, have cut her down with the empty bucket in her hands while her father was drawing water. Hesitation kills, Paulus thought.

"What are the wizards like?" she asked.

"They are wizards," Paulus said. "Not like men. But not cruel."

"How long until we get there?"

"A little while yet," Paulus said. He was silent after that, and they rode the edge of a canyon in which night fell early and forced them to make camp while the sky above was still light.

At times, Paulus knew, he was slow to apprehend the consequences of his actions. Now he realized that he had complicated his task first by concocting a story and then by taking the girl. She was one of the apprentice's six; Myros might well know that Paulus had her, and if he also knew about the boy he might be provoked into retaliation. Better to have killed her quickly and ridden on. Regardless of the wizard's injunction, Paulus could not afford to carry her with him in his pursuit of Myros. Nor could he return her, now that his mouth had run away with his reason and pronounced that she might be returned if she did not satisfy the wizards. He could easily imagine what such a stigma might mean to a child in a place like Branchefort Valley. He stirred Philo's eggs over the fire and damned himself for losing sight of his task.

Over the sound of the night breeze in the canyon, he heard Sophia crying quietly. End this, he thought, and rose into a crouch.

"I'm afraid," she said, and the sound of her voice destroyed his resolve. He sat next to her. Paulus had no knowledge of children. He had none of his own and had been taken from his own home at about Sophia's age, leaving behind three younger sisters whom he had never seen again.

"Never been out of the valley before?" he asked her.

She shook her head and wiped at her nose before tearing a piece of bread from the loaf and scooping eggs out of the bowl. Cowardice was a thick, bitter syrup in Paulus' throat. The boy with the stick in his hand had fallen without a sound, face still bearing traces of his smile at seeing Paulus' sword—yet Paulus knew that in the dying reaches of the boy's brain had been the knowledge of his murder. He found that he could not bear the idea of Sophia dying with that same knowledge. Her name, he thought. If I had not learned her name . . .

"Let me tell you a story," Paulus said, and then he fell silent because he couldn't remember any stories. He remembered the sound of his father's voice telling him stories when he was a small boy, but he couldn't hear any of the words. "There was a little girl who dreamed that she was a bird," he began, and he let his voice follow the idea of that bird until Sophia was asleep. In the morning he buried the crusts of the bread with her, and burned the coat over her grave. As he climbed out of the canyon into sunlight, a wind sharp with snow raised gooseflesh on his arms. He filled his lungs and held his breath until the edges of his vision faded into red, then exhaled slowly, slowly, feeling his mind start to fade. At the point of unconsciousness he let himself breathe again, deeply and freely. He did not remember where he had learned the exercise, but it cleared his mind, and as his horse—Brown—picked his way across frosted scree below a peak like the head of a boil, Paulus let his mind wander. During the short time he had slept the night before, he had dreamed of being a dog, in a warm room with thick rugs and two great stone chairs too high for him to leap onto. There had been a kind woman and an old, old man, and another man who would not look at him but spoke gently. *O queen,* he thought; and after that, *O brother.*

The motion of a hare bounding between rocks drew his attention. He slipped an old throwing knife from its sheath at the small of his back and waited for it to move again, thinking that now he was over the first high ridge of peaks and in this expanse of alpine valleys, game would be more plentiful. In the high country, above treeline, was nothing but pikas and the occasional adventuresome goat. He wished he had brought a bow, but the truth was that no one had ever mistaken him for a skillful archer; his boyhood circus training, though, had served him well where knives were concerned. When the hare made its move, Paulus flicked his wrist. Simple. Five minutes later, the hare was dressed and dangling from his saddle. He rode on, trying not to think of sopping up the hare's fat with Sophia's bread. Skill with knives or no, Paulus knew that hunger was going to be a close companion as he moved farther from settled regions. The hermits and occasional isolated hamlets huddled in the valleys would not all be as hospitable as the Brancheforts had been.

Sparser settlement also meant that it would be harder to track Myros—although Myros would have his own problems, chief among them finding four more children to collect. Paulus had no doubt that all six of Myros' collection would be children, and the certainty had come so quietly that he was reluctant to examine it too closely. He mistrusted his own intuition, feeling that it was often fueled by whatever it was he had paid the wizard to make him forget, and he feared breaking the spell by looking too closely at the workings of his mind.

There was the problem, too, of where Myros was going—and why. Moving north as fast as feet could carry him, moving deeper and deeper into the winter that had already left the lowlands, Myros fled as if frantic to go backwards in time. If he kept heading north, he would reach the marshes and tundras that gave onto the ice-choked Mare Ultima. What would Myros want with the tribes who followed the whales and caribou?

A stirring in Paulus' mind set his fingers tingling with more than the cold. *I can block the memories of your mind,* the wizard had said, *but the body's memories are beyond my reach.* Paulus looked at his hands and wondered what they remembered. He had paid good silver for his forgetfulness, but no wizard had yet charmed the curiosity out of man or woman, or the desire. Paulus' brother was ample evidence of that.

2

Days passed, and fell from memory with the sunset. Paulus saw no one, and stopped remembering his dreams. He was well into the second range of mountains, leading Brown on a foot trail skirting snow-buried canyons, when he found the apprentice's third. He saw smoke funneling out of a crevice on the canyon wall, and found a cave entrance below it. Calling in, he roused an old hermit and described Myros. "Yes," the hermit nodded, and invited Paulus in for hot water and flat bread. "He was here. And yes, he spoke to my lad and moved on. Quite a soft one to be this deep in the mountains."

Paulus thought, but did not say, that there were many kinds of hardness.

"And he would not eat, nor drink," the hermit went on. Paulus watched his fingers, how they moved through the silent catechism of the hermit's god. Nine beads on a catgut string, a sacred abacus ticking off the arithmetic of holiness. I will pray after, Paulus thought. Not now.

"I thank you for your welcome," he said.

The hermit did not acknowledge this. "Wizards," he grumbled, and spat into the fire.

"Myros is not yet a wizard," Paulus said. "I am sent to make sure he never will be."

In the hermit's eyes, Paulus saw suspicion. And something else; their expression teased at a memory, irritating like a hair on the back of the tongue. Eyes like gray stones, they put him in mind of something, stirred echoes of a kind of love that he could not remember feeling since he was a boy.

"If you are following him," the hermit said, "what does it matter whether he spoke to my lad?"

You have not been gone from inhabited places as long as all that, old man, thought Paulus. "I need to know if he is collecting," he said, and might have said more but the hermit threw hot water in his face and at the same time someone caught hold of his hair from behind. He threw a forearm across his throat and felt the impact of the blade, and then burning as the hermit kicked the embers of the fire across his leggings. Paulus scissored his legs, scattering the coals back toward the hermit, and with his left hand gripped the wrist of whoever had hold of his hair. The blade caught him on the cheek, and with an animal roar he squeezed until he felt bones snap. The grip on his hair loosened, and he pivoted to his feet, twisting the arm and breaking it again before he saw that he held a long-haired boy of perhaps thirteen, face twisted with hate and fear and pain. Paulus let him go, and the boy sprang up with the knife again. Stepping to his right, Paulus slapped the knife hand down and punched the boy hard on the left temple, knocking him straight down into the packed-earth floor, where he lay motionless save for a slow movement of his lips.

Looking over his shoulder, Paulus saw the hermit brandishing a burning branch. I have tried lies, and I have tried truth, he thought. This time he did not speak at all.

The next morning, in the sunny mouth of a snow cave near a frozen creek, Paulus ran his fingers carefully along his wounds. He had done this the night before, but could not credit what his fingertips reported. His cheek was unmarked, though his tongue felt a chipped molar where the thrust of the boy's blade had landed, and on his forearm a deep cut ran for three inches or so, then stopped for slightly more, then began again before tapering into a scratch near the outside of his elbow. Paulus probed the skin between the two cuts as he reconstructed the fight in his mind. One blow across the arm, one blow to the cheek, then he had turned. Could he have forgotten a third strike? It seemed impossible. The uncut skin felt normal to the touch, but when he pressed the point of a knife into it, he could not leave a mark. An odd smell filled his nostrils, raising the hair on his forearms and shrinking his testicles though he could not identify it and did not know why he should be afraid. The forgetting, he thought. Perhaps the body cannot forget any more than a bird can forget to fly south.

Well. Put it from your mind, he told himself. You paid for the forgetting, and must have had a good reason.

More important was the fact that Myros knew he was being pursued. The hermit's ambush made that clear, and that meant that at the time Paulus had killed the boy on the farm, Myros had not yet collected the hermit's acolyte. So, Paulus reasoned, I am closing on him, but he will have laid traps where time and circumstances allow. Hesitation kills, and even more fatal is the failure to learn from mistakes. Three of Myros' collection remained. Each, no doubt, would pose more risk than the last—and Myros himself could not be underestimated. The time for a budding wizard to gather his collection came near the end of his studies, when he could go no further without the actual performance of magic. Together, the sparks of magic in each of the six merged into a wizard's strength, and in fact his life, since a wizard lived only as long as one of his collection survived. Paulus wasn't sure which would be more difficult, eliminating the six or confronting Myros after he had completed his collection. The apprentice would not have completed his studies, but he would have learned enough in the Agate Tower to be a difficult opponent.

Paulus had killed wizards before. He could do it again. He could also fail, and although he did not fear death, he feared dying and believed that knowledge of the difference between the two was the true wellspring of courage. Having taken money from the wizards' guild, however, Paulus knew better than to abandon his mission. He finished the flat bread he had taken from the hermit's cave, and gnawed the last of the rabbit, and went on.

He came to tundra, and found a thin track that followed the course of a north-flowing river. Memories threatened, and Paulus held his breath until they went away. Five days he walked, eating little and haunted by the prospect of remembering. Often he thought of his brother, dead these four years, and of the strange sacrifice his brother had made. More often still he thought of the king whose father had killed Paulus' father, and who had taken Paulus into his service and transformed him from an acrobat into the man he now was. Something slippery and vast remained just out of reach in his mind, and although he fought the impulse he could not help grasping after it. Nor could he help tracking his fingers across the blank patch of skin between the two healing cuts, or the bearded cheek that had not parted for the acolyte's dagger. The magic is faltering, he thought, and was glad that he might be whole again but afraid that he might find his failures more complete as well.

A village of thatched huts hugged the sandy inside of a bend in the river. Four men came out to meet him, careful not to point their spears too directly at him, and speaking a language that Paulus knew only in fragments from fellow soldiers. They recognized the sigil of the king on the hilt of his sword, and the figure of the Agate Tower on the medallion tied to Brown's bridle, and when he asked about the apprentice who wore a ring over his glove they nodded and pointed to a lean-to of driftwood and sod downstream of the village.

When he knocked at the crooked sticks of the door, it fell in, and before Paulus could draw his sword he was set upon by dogs. A ringing rose in his ears and he killed them, one at a time while the others tore at his legs and leapt snarling at his face. Before they were all dead a spear struck a glancing blow across the back of his head; Paulus caught the last dog, ran it through, and used its body as a shield to catch the thrust of the next spear. He twisted the dog's body, jerking the spear from the hands of the villager who had held it, and killed him. The other three spread into a semicircle around him. Blood warm on the back of his neck, Paulus said, "He was dead when Myros came here and you did not set your dogs on him. Where is he?"

The answer was three spears, driven at once toward his gut. He stepped to his left, between two of them, and struck down the two villagers before they could regain their balance. "You're not killing caribou now," Paulus said to the last of them. "Leave off."

It wasn't working. Paulus looked into the last man's face and saw a look he had come to know well in his days with the king's army. May I never come to the point, he prayed, when I am willing to die for the sake of not being shamed by my failure to kill myself uselessly. A shouting pierced the ringing in his ears, and he looked to his left, upstream, where an old man and a younger woman stood with two children, a boy and a girl. Naked. Twins. The children stared wide-eyed at Paulus, streaked in blood and holding the carcass of a dog. They stared at the three dead men sprawled around him, and at the dead dogs fanning out from the open doorway of the driftwood lean-to. Their expressions did not change as the elder, standing behind them and looking Paulus in the eye, held up a bone knife and cut their throats before the eyes of the village. First the girl, then the boy, knelt and looked down at the blood running down their bellies. They put their hands over their wounds. The boy coughed, and sucked in a huge breath before choking blood out of his mouth. The girl's mouth opened and her tongue came out as if she had tasted something bad. Then both of them, almost at once, put out a bloody hand to the ground and used it to guide their bodies down to rest.

Something broke inside Paulus. The ringing in his ears disappeared, and he lowered his sword. "They were dead when Myros came," he repeated. "I am made the instrument of his madness."

In the woman's eyes was something neither pity nor hate. "Go," the woman said.

Many children I have let live, Paulus thought that night. Other men might have killed them all.

And still other men, he answered himself, would have returned the wizards' money before killing the boy with the stick.

Again he grasped after the easy justification: Once Myros collected them, they were going to die. Baby turtles. Paulus had been kinder about it than most would have. Still and yet, there were men who made their way in the world without killing children. Paulus prayed to one day be among them.

One more. He lay looking at the northern stars, knowing that some baby turtles survived, and thinking: One more.

And on into the country of stone and smoke and ice, where men ate seals and great bears ate men. The world is running out of land, Paulus thought. The sixth cannot be far. After the hermit's trap and the ambush laid at the village, he was no longer traveling, but patrolling, eyes and ears sharpened for possible threats, right hand moving restlessly back and forth between Brown's saddle horn and the pommel of his sword. He caught himself praying under his breath, and wondered with wry humor if this was what it took for him to discover piety. Also he had the feeling that the membrane of his forgetting was growing dangerously thin, as if the part of his mind veiled by magic was speaking to him, more loudly and insistently with each hour he traveled north.

I have been here before, he thought—and held his breath until the world grew purplish at the edges and he felt himself swaying in the saddle.

On a morning sharp with ocean breeze and the smells of northern plants awakening to the promise of summer's endless days, Paulus came upon a farmer plowing. Pulling his own blade, the man bent to his work, shirtless and running with sweat even in the chill air. Paulus rode to him, sword drawn and leveled. When the farmer looked up, he asked, "Has a young man with a ring over his glove passed this way?"

The farmer let the handles of his plow drop and squinted up at Paulus. "It's you," he said.

Paulus raised his sword, and would have killed the farmer except the man spoke his name. "How do you know my name?" he asked. "Was it Myros who told you?"

"Do you—it hasn't been that long."

"Since what?"

The farmer cocked his head. "You don't remember me, either, do you? Will?"

"Why would I?"

"Oh," the farmer—Will—said. "You had a magic done, didn't you?"

Paulus' sword point dipped in Will's direction.

"Paulus," Will said. "Your apprentice was here, yesterday, and he did collect a boy. But there's more you need to know."

"No, there isn't," Paulus said. "I don't know how you know me, or if you know me or if Myros left you this part to play. None of that matters. Take me to the boy."

"Well, I was going to do that," Will said. "After all, he's yours."

The membrane stretched thinner, and then Will added, "From Joy. When you came to kill the dragon."

And Paulus remembered.

When he tried to sleep, he heard the dragon.

The whisper of its scales, their soft scrape and rattle. The cold draft of its indrawn breath, so like the breath of a cave. The slow creak of its wings, unfolding in the dark. All memory now, the ghost of his bitter triumph scratching its way through the inside of his mind.

He rolled over, felt the mattress under him: so soft, softer than the wintry mountainside where he'd camped the night before he'd gone into the dragon's lair. In a corner of his chamber, a mouse scampered. There were hours yet before dawn.

He threw back the sheet and stood. In the courtyard below his window, the bucket hung over the well swung in the night wind. A light shone in the stables, and Paulus shrugged into a robe. The groom, Andrew, rarely slept and had grown accustomed to Paulus' intrusions in the middle of the night.

Before going down to the stables, Paulus rummaged in the dark for the bottle on his nightstand. Better to bring a gift when interrupting another man's solitude.

Andrew looked up at the squeak of the stable door's hinges. "Paulus," he said. Paulus set the bottle on the square table Andrew used to cut tack, and the old groom grinned. "The dragon again," he said.

Paulus sat heavily on the cutting bench.

Killing the dragon: the shock of the blade driven at an angle below the scales behind its shoulder, the scalding spray of blood over his hands and face (no blade can cut his face now, nor a long irregular patch of skin on the inside of his right forearm where the seam of his jerkin had split), the long ropes of skin and muscle hanging from Paulus' flanks and legs where its claws had raked him, the sight of his own bones. And then the woman who put him on a sledge and dragged him to her hearth, where the winter passed into spring without him remembering, and in the spring when he was strong again he desired her, and would have taken her back to The Fells; but although she gave freely of her body and her love, she would not leave her birthplace. So he had come back, and slept little and drunk much, and spent the dying hours of the night with Andrew at the tack bench, until with the last of the bounty on the dragon he had purchased his forgetting.

• • •

Paulus woke.

In her language, her name meant Joy. She had had one man before him, killed the year before hunting the horned whales among the ice floes of the Mare Ultima. Perhaps she had had none after.

He could remember the smell of the cutting bench as if it were in the room with him. The morning after sharing that last bottle with Andrew, he had gone to a spell broker and negotiated the terms of his forgetting. Now he remembered it all again: The pain that crept like worms under his skin as the dragon's poison did its slow work, the way the screams had fought their way out of his mouth as she dragged him down the hillside and for miles along the riverside trail. The pungency of her remedies, and the spasms of his body as they drew the poisons out. The long silences in her house, broken only by the whickering of the wind in the thatched roof—and at last the moment when he had caught her hand and said, *Come to me.*

The boy, Paulus thought. The boy now sleeping on his pallet near the farmer's hearth. He could be mine.

I want him to be mine.

He could never have imagined himself feeling this. He felt newly full, spilling over, as if the unstoppering of his memory had scoured away other walls. Paulus sat up, sealskin covers falling away from him. He had spoken to the boy the day before, Will hanging back with more discretion than Paulus would have expected. A simple conversation, and when the boy had asked in his pidgin four-year-old way to see Paulus' sword, Paulus knew he did not have it in him to kill this boy. Perhaps it was the fact that he might be killing his own offspring—though that had not stopped a number of men Paulus had known, and even admired—and perhaps it was simply the lesson of this journey. The Book of the god to whom Paulus prayed spoke of the Journey, and the Lesson. Part of Paulus' attraction to this faith was his life's own journeying, the travels and travails; now here was a chapter of the Book incarnate in these four limbs, these two eyes and small voice. The boy did not know that Paulus might be his father. Will had not been so bold. Paulus wanted to tell him, and he burned on the forks of a problem. Duty spoke with the voice he had always heeded; the dawning reality of kinship, and the small hope he held of being able to face his maker, spoke in quietly unanswerable opposition.

Paulus remembered sunrises slanting in through the cobwebby windows of Andrew's tack shed. Had Andrew ever seen Paulus on the streets of The Fells, thought to hail him perhaps? Had he told Andrew of his plan to buy the forgetting?

The sun was not yet up. Will was moving around just outside the door, and Paulus could hear the deep, even breaths of the boy. His boy. The sixth of Myros' collection.

Paulus stretched. He had not slept under a roof in more than a month, and his body was aging past the point when it could easily absorb a month on the campaign. The scars along his ribs hurt, and his shoulders popped, and in an instant of quiet revelation he understood that Myros had collected children, and Paulus had killed them, because Myros wanted the dragon Paulus had killed four years before.

Will had a copy of the Book on a tree-stump table beside his hearth. It was still too dark to read, but Paulus paged through the Book anyway, soothing himself with the beads in his fingers and the familiar weight and texture of the faith he had known all his life. He thought he was looking for something in the Book, but he did not know what, and when enough light had returned to the sky that he could discern the words, he set the Book aside and went to his saddlebag for whetstone and oil.

Sharpening his sword, Paulus imagined the boy grown into a soldier, and was filled with a black fury at what the world had done to him. No, he thought. The boy slept as only a child can, still as death, unstirred by the scrape of the whetstone. Memories rode in on the tide of Paulus' anger. In the Book was a story of a girl named Lily, saved by a story whispered in her ear while she was sleeping. Thinking of it, Paulus found his own tongue loosening. A story came to him, and as he remembered it he told it to the boy.

3

Legend had it that the commoners' gift of magic came from the gods' anger at the separation of people into high and low. Like all legends, this one was as good an explanation as any, and the kingdom largely subscribed to it. One bit of magic, to be deployed once and only once, whether foolish or wise: this was the commoner's reward for a lifetime of subservience. The jester found this delicious, and wasted no opportunity to crow over the kingdom's fatuous belief. But the jester had secrets, and reasons.

Much of his life was apparent in the topology of his face. The king's common subjects bore an expression of calm security, a faith in their sovereign and in their one bit of magic to see them through whatever demands life would place upon them. But as if he had been built by one of the angry gods, the jester's face quirked and twisted with freshly remembered regret, and his cast eye, forever looking vacantly away to his right, took on a horrible aspect when his humor turned scabrous and biting. The younger princes and princesses fled the throne room at his every entrance, pushing each other in most ignoble haste, and the queen reluctantly took action when the youngest prince, awakening in mortal fear from a nightmare of the jester's crooked eye and whiplash tongue, ran blindly from his room and broke both of his legs in a fall down a flight of stairs.

Only a few hours later, in the throne room, the queen looked sadly from her liege lord to his *memento mori,* telling each that the safety of the royal progeny outweighed decades of service and reward. "His loyalty to you speaks well of him," she said to the king. "Even your dog is not so loyal."

The old dog looked up at her, the tip of his tail twitching. The jester thought that if he had had a tail, it might have twitched as well.

The queen spoke more than she knew, and behind his beard the king mused. The jester farted outrageously and refused to say a word, but within the scrawny rack of his chest, his heart beat with both fear and love for the queen who at that moment was proposing that he be pensioned off to a mountain barony safely away from tender gazes. His love for her exceeded the bounds even of his love for ruler and kingdom, and in that moment the jester bitterly regretted the day when he had loosed his one bit of magic to save the king.

Outside the castle walls, the jester sat crosslegged against a dead tree, looking out over the shore of a lake whose surface was rippled like an old window. He was tired of conjuring witty deflating comments. Tired of handstands, tired of juggling the skulls of the king's would-be assassins. He'd grown old, found aches in his joints and sleepless nights at the end of every day. There were many things he wished had never happened.

The jester had not always been a jester, any more than the king had been a king or the king's dog had been a dog. The day the old king died, the crown prince sat a silent vigil by his father's body until midnight, when he leapt to his feet and went to the chamber door. "Tomorrow a barred door closes on me," he said to his guard. "Tonight I walk through my city."

In the marketplace the uncrowned king walked among his subjects. He flirted with shop girls, bought perhaps one too many flagons of wine, and found himself in the shadow of the city walls watching a pair of ragged street performers. They were tired and performed reluctantly, but he gave them the strength of gold thrown at their feet. When the first birds had begun to chirp in anticipation of the dawn, the pair of acrobats were still turning their tumbles and mining their repertoire for tricks this munificent stranger had not yet seen.

Few things travel faster then news of a king's death, and the two weary acrobats were attuned to town gossip as only itinerant clowns can be. The older brother had absorbed the news and let it find a resting place in his mind; the younger had grown consumed with desire to avenge an injustice perpetrated by the dead king many years before, when an unlucky circus ringmaster had made an inopportune comment about the old king's cleft palate. One thing that travels faster than news of royal death is tidings of royal insult, and before long the ringmaster had vanished into the castle dungeon as his two boys performed with masklike faces before their sovereign, who rose at the end to pronounce the show the most excellent he'd seen in many a year.

The older son had made his peace with this. One lived in one's world, and one did not insult the king. The younger, though, turned the injustice inward and fed on it, not realizing that it was also feeding on him. Over a span of ten years man and hatred grew more to look like one another, and at last on a breezy summer night with dew on the ivy that climbed the city walls, the younger brother, addled with fantasies of regicide, saw his chance for revenge.

It would be their final routine, the brothers told their sole watcher. Dawn was coming, and besides they knew no trick to better it.

The uncrowned king accepted this. "I have been well entertained," he said, "and who better than you to know when you have no more to give?"

Nodding, the brothers unfolded a leather package containing ten knives. "Ready?" the older asked.

"We should rehearse it once."

"Start with three, then."

The king couldn't be certain whether the clowns were really so uncertain of this routine, or whether the uncertainty was part of their patter. Predawn gleam flashed on the knife blades as they flickered between the two brothers in a pattern almost intelligible. "Marvelous," the king said. "I imagine that's dangerous given your eye. Can you see out of it?"

Only for a moment, an eyeblink or even less, a long-dormant sense of hurt bloomed in the older brother. His life had given him a keen sense of irony, and it never escaped his notice when audiences tossed comments toward him of the sort that had gotten his father killed. The pain passed almost immediately, but not before causing a tremor in his throwing hand.

Blades clashed as the younger brother knocked the errant throw from the air. "Careful, brother," he said. The older brother blinked.

"Well enough," he lied. "I see well enough."

Six knives again, this time flawless for thirty seconds. Then the younger brother said, "Now four. Now." Together they stooped, and the gleaming pattern between them recomplicated itself just long enough for the king to think *Masterful*. Then the younger brother cried out and dropped his knives in a clatter. One of them bounded toward the king, who reached to pick it up.

"Not to worry, Your Majesty," the younger brother said. He stooped to retrieve the knife, and just as it registered in the king's mind that this slim and smiling trickster knew who he was — had watched him from crowds since he was old enough to assume the paste crown of First Successor — the younger brother leaned in low and thrust the knife into the king's belly.

What should have followed then was a lingering death and a hasty scampering escape over the city walls, but the uncrowned king was not quite the fool the younger acrobat had thought him. His mail shirt, forged within subterranean earshot of the cell where the old ringmaster had died wishing for sunlight, caught the blade and held it with only an inch of its tip parting skin and muscle. The younger brother's weight bore the king over, and he lay on his back, struggling to catch his breath and looking calmly into the eyes of his assassin.

"This blood," the younger brother said, holding his cut hand so the blood dripped onto the king's face. "It is my father's, and I will avenge it." He drew another knife from his belt.

"You are older than I am," the king said. "I do not know your father. Your grievance is with a dead man."

"When you are dead," the younger brother said, "I will have no grievance." He planted one knee in the king's chest. His brother called his name.

"Kill me, then," said the king. "But know that you redress no wrong. You kill as a mad dog kills, because you don't know what else to do."

Perhaps the younger brother hesitated for a moment, or perhaps magic saw its opportunity and spoke through his elder sibling's mouth; but before the knife could fall the older brother said, "You will not be a mad dog, brother. You will not repay shame with shame."

With those words, his life's one bit of magic whirlpooled from his body, and where a moment before the king had lain helpless under an assassin's knife, now the older brother watched as a small brown dog pawed at the king's tunic and strained to lick his chin.

The king pushed the dog aside and with a disgusted noise jerked the knife from the broken links of his mail. "Did you know who I was?" he asked.

The remaining brother, three knives in his two dangling hands, shook his head.

"It is odd," the king said, and had to pause for breath. He struggled to his feet. "To thank a man who would turn his brother into a dog."

"Odder yet to save the son of the man who killed my father," the older brother replied.

The king looked from the older brother to the attentive dog, who limped ever so slightly on one front paw. "So," he said.

"But I have seen men die, and few were able to face it as you did," the older brother went on. He began to gather up his props and gimmicks. "I thought I saw a kingly man in you." He tried to say something more, but he could not speak of what he had done.

The dog sat in front of the king. His tail wagged against one of the fallen knives, and he started up at the clatter and ran a few steps before returning with tail and nose both low to the ground. "Take care of my brother," said the lone acrobat as he shouldered his pack. "I see he wishes to remain with you."

"Why should I not kill him?"

The acrobat looked the king in the eye. "Your grievance is not with a dog."

Dawn broke on the castle's highest towers.

"True," said the king. "Very well, he will remain with me. As will you. I will have you and your brother at my throne, one to remind me of how close to death I came, and the other to remind me of why I was allowed to live. Walk with me, king's jester."

All of this was bad enough; but then the jester fell in love with the queen.

He remembered the moment of falling in love like a story told by someone else. The great stones of the hall outside the throne room, pale gray except streaks on either side, where generations of the royal wolfhounds had rubbed their ears along the grooves and ridges in the ancient stones. This king, whose life the jester had saved, was the first in memory to keep a limping brown dog of anonymous pedigree instead of the great loping hounds named for stars and mythical ancestors.

Passing her in the hall: she taller by a head and younger by two generations, he favoring a heel bruised earlier that day tumbling for an ambassador. She with hair the color of the old streaks in the walls, a brown almost black, and eyes the color of the untouched stones, the gray of a cloud heavy with lightning; he with a balding head and knuckles swollen by winter's chill. The jester became exalted in that moment, realizing that she was the castle, she was the kingdom, it was the twin example of her kindness and her iron rectitude that made it possible for the king to spare the jester's brother. He loved her because she seemed in that moment to him like an ideal given flesh, an ideal for which the sacrifice of a brother was not too great. Foolish, yes, and sentimental: but as good an explanation as any.

It haunted the jester that he had been willing to kill his brother. And he had; only the fickleness of magic had sped his mouth and stayed his hand. He found some small comfort in the royal heir's person, his utter lack of resemblance to his father. The old king had been capricious, vindictive, wanton in both kindness and cruelty. His successor remained scrupulous and fair, even generous. Around him the kingdom prospered without war.

And I didn't kill my brother, the jester thought. I saved him. I protected him, as an older brother must.

The king's dog was old now, gray around the muzzle and lame in his hind legs. A superstition arose that the king would live only as long as his dog (no one said this about the jester), and although the king knew better, still he protected the dog's life as jealously as his own, lest its death provoke unrest in the kingdom. The irony of this kept the jester in fine form for the mordant humor expected of him at court.

What would happen, he wondered, if the king were actually persuaded to foist him off on some rustic baron? Sooner or later, wouldn't the story of the dog his brother leak between the royal lips? And wouldn't the queen . . . ? The duty of her heart was to her husband, and of her mind to her king. She would have the dog killed out of a kind of loathing mercy, pitying the beast its lost humanity even as she ordered it drowned to ensure that no entombed memory would resurface and tear out the throat of the sleeping king.

Having once thought this, the jester grew certain events could play out no other way, just as having once seen the queen as his own ideals bodied forth he could never rid himself of his passion for her. Exaltation fled him. "Why must I love her?" he demanded of the sky, but the clouds of course took on the color of her eyes and kept their peace. Love twisted inside him the way magic had on its way from his body, anguish and ecstasy. Loving the queen who would kill his brother, the jester could only think of her implacable magnificence, her mind like light in cold water.

It was afternoon. The jester left the lake, went back to the city and the castle, and the next day the queen mentioned it again. Wouldn't the old jester be happier away from the trials and pressures of court? she asked, slipping through the fissure in his field of vision, and the jester knew what he had to do.

The spell broker kept himself secret, but the jester knew where to find him in the twilit side of the city. "My magic is gone," the jester said.

"Else why would you be here?" the broker said, and displayed brown teeth in a round white face shaved smooth as an egg. "Let me look at you."

The jester kept himself still as the spell broker plucked a strand of his hair and burned it over a candle, traced the outline of his ribs, smelled his breath, looked into his eyes and ears. "What is it you want?" the broker said upon finishing his inspection.

"The safety of my brother." The jester had heard stories about the deviousness of the spell broker. It was best not to be too specific too soon.

"Safety. Magic cannot guarantee safety. Magic can sometimes kill a threat, perhaps redirect it. Forgetting-magic is the easiest, though, and the surest."

She could forget, the jester thought. It made him inexplicably sad, though, the idea of court whispers: the queen, forget? She of the searchlight mind and unshakable will, the grey eyes like stones that held within them memories of each and every soul who passed by?

I will protect my brother.

"Forgetting magic, yes," the jester said. "If it is the easiest, it must come cheaply."

"The cheapest magic comes dear," said the broker.

"Name your price."

"Your eye."

"Very well," the jester said, and in a sudden panic thought *too soon, spoke too soon,* because the broker was still speaking, and the words out of his mouth were, "Your left eye."

My good eye, the jester thought. How will I look on the queen?

But his mouth was already open saying yes.

He found he could look upon the queen, after a fashion. If he positioned himself correctly, she would, on her way to kiss the king, walk through the part of his world that had not faded to a lifeless fog. He could not see her clearly, only well enough to remember how she had once appeared to him.

Well enough.

I did this for you, he would whisper sometimes under his breath. *So you would not feel betrayed when you discovered what I have done for my brother.*

In the jester's thirty-seventh year, when the dog his brother was thirty-three, the king had retired him from acrobatics, and the jester passed his days in excremental assaults on courtiers even as he kept his head turned slightly away to the left of the queen. The court thought him blind in the right eye instead of the left, and grudgingly credited him for his seemly deference to the queen's presence. They imagined that this deference arose out of gratitude at being permitted to remain at court, and the queen's stature increased among the aristocratic gossips, her reputation for kindness burnishing the well-known brilliance of her mind and the much-praised symmetry of her face. She often stooped to pet the old dog, who would thump his tail against the leg of the throne at her approach.

The jester kept his secrets, and he was careful around the children. The broker's spell made no guarantee against the queen's remembering. If he pitied himself from time to time, he ran his fingers where the queen's had been, along the dog his brother's neck, and he said to himself, unable to stop: *One lives in one's world*, he said to the sleeping dog. *One lives in one's world*.

4

The boy still slept. But Will had come in from outside. "You're not blind," he said.

"I'm not a dog, either," Paulus said. He set Will's copy of the Book aside.

Will lit his pipe. "Twice someone spent their magic on you?"

"Aye," Paulus said. "Twice."

"And how did the second come about?"

"You wouldn't believe me," Paulus said.

"Already I don't believe you," Will said. "Tell another one."

"My brother confessed to the queen and as a reward for the laughter he had brought to the court, she bought me back my shape as a man, on the condition that I enter the king's service. I fought eleven years in the king's wars, and then he sent me to kill the dragon. When I came back, my brother and the king had both died, and I was released. Since then I have been for hire."

Will blew smoke rings over the sleeping boy. "All of this after you tried to kill the king? Ha," he said. "I wish that was true. No, I don't."

Three times, actually, Paulus thought. The forgetting he'd bought four years ago in The Fells was the third. Paulus made an occasional pastime of imagining who that little bit of magic had come from: a gambler needing to cover a debt, a soldier wanting a woman, a merchant whose cargo had foundered in the straits. Perhaps even the woman who had borne this child who might be his. The brokers of The Fells moved through the hamlets and farms of the mountains, following the lucrative scents of poverty and desperation. Their prices weren't fair, but even a rapacious deal often made the difference between feeding children and selling them.

"Three years ago?" he asked.

"Four, in the fall."

"How?"

Will shrugged. "She was bringing water. Sat down for a rest beside the path, I guess, and I found her when I heard the boy crying. Maybe six months old, he was."

Could be, Paulus thought. The sleeping boy was curled on his side, arms drawn in under his chin, still shadowed from the sunlight falling through the hut's single window. Firelight glowed in the tangles of his hair. Paulus thought he might see something of himself in the shape of the boy's shoulders, the line of his jaw.

Today I must kill Myros, he thought. Because if I do not, I will have to kill this boy, and I cannot.

"Have you named him? Had she?"

"She called him after you," Will said. "So I did, too."

Paulus was brimful and shattering. A boy with my name, he thought. After all this, all the leavings and the years with no place to call my own, in my fiftieth year I ride out on a mission of killing and find a boy with my name.

It was written in the Book: *Let the Lesson be.*

He stood, and his knees cracked. "Today this ends," Paulus said. "One way or another. If the boy asks for me, tell him I will return by nightfall or not at all."

The boy. Still, Paulus admonished himself, you cannot call him by his name?

He walked the final steps of his Agate Tower errand, his body leading him to the dragon's cave as if his scars were lines on a map. It would have taken Myros some time to prepare the spell to control the dragon, and more time yet for him to gather his courage and enter the cave when the dragon did not come out. Quite a string of surprises Myros was in for, Paulus thought, and bared his teeth as he wound up a switchbacking footpath that ended on the ridge above the cave. He made no effort to disguise his presence. If Myros had already spent his energy on the spell, then he was just another baby turtle; if he had not,

Paulus was in for a hard fight, but on this day he would kill no man from behind. He crested the ridge and closed his eyes, riding out a wave of memories. The cave mouth, like a half-lidded eye, was the same, yet it seemed smaller to him; the smell of the snow on the north side of the ridge made him think of ice storms rattling against a window with a sound like the rasp of the dragon's scales.

They were all before him now, the specters of those gone from his life: his brother, Andrew, his mother, the king. Men he had served with. Joy. And the boy she had named for him.

When Paulus opened his eyes, Myros was looking at him from the cave entrance. "For this you made me kill children," Paulus said.

"I made you do nothing," Myros said, and made a gesture with his ringed hand.

Paulus was alight with pain: every blade that had ever cut him cut him anew. He felt the teeth of dogs and the dragon's talons, the piercing of an arrow and the grate of a spearpoint across his skull. Thumbs gouged at his eyes, and bootheels ground his fingers. He dropped his sword and felt his knees buckle. Blood roared in his ears, and somewhere beyond it he heard Myros' footsteps on the stones of the trail. Looking up through tears, he saw the apprentice coming nearer. You misjudge me, Paulus thought, and drank of his pain until it had given him strength to stand, and when he had gotten to his feet he left his sword where it lay and fell upon Myros with bare hands.

When it was done, he lay gasping on the stony ground as the apprentice's spell slowly faded from his body. He felt as if he was being knit together again, and when the pain had faded into the leaden dullness that for Paulus always followed killing, he got to his feet. Leaving his sword where it lay, he walked a short distance into the cave, to the point where the light from without finally failed. Trailing away into the dark, the bones of the dragon had already begun taking on the color of the stones around them.

One more, Paulus remembered thinking. I was right, and I was wrong.

It was afternoon when he returned to Will's farm. The boy was on his hands and knees following an insect through the beaten grass. He looked up at Paulus' approach and stood. "There's a beetle there," he said.

Paulus knew in that moment how little he understood of children, and how enormous his task was. "Your name is Paulus. Is that right?" he asked.

The boy nodded, but his attention was already wandering back to the beetle. He parted the grasses looking for it.

"My name is Paulus too."

The boy looked over his shoulder at Paulus. Where, Paulus wondered? A place without wizards. A place without these bargains driven for your soul. A place where my boy will not follow my path. He realized he had forgotten his sword, and resolved that he would never wear another. Let the Lesson be.

"You're going to come with me," Paulus said.

And the boy said, "Where are we going?"

First published in *The Magazine of Fantasy & Science Fiction*, June 2007.

ABOUT THE AUTHOR

Alexander Irvine has written more than thirty books. His most recent original novel is *Buyout,* while on the licensed front he has recently written novelizations of *Pacific Rim* and *Dawn of the Planet of the Apes,* as well as *The Secret Journal of Ichabod Crane,* for the television show *Sleepy Hollow.* He also writes the online games *Marvel Avengers Alliance, Marvel War of Heroes,* and *Marvel Puzzle Quest.* A native of Ypsilanti, Michigan, he lives in Maine but still roots for the Tigers.

I Sing the Lady Electric
BRIAN FRANCIS SLATTERY

Science fiction has been a thread running through black music in America at least since jazz pianist Sun Ra's vision of a trip to Saturn as a college student in the late 1930s. Sun Ra might be considered the archetype that later musicians have followed. The twin themes of oppressive social alienation and ecstatic personal liberation run deep in both his music and his lyrics. As he had players chant about flying to other planets, he also asked them to play without much regard for conventional ideas of tonality or harmony. Where some ears would find dissonance, confusion, or cacophony in his music and his message, he found transcendence. And he wore the outlandish costumes to prove it.

Sun Ra was controversial at first, but he lived long enough to see others pick up the same thread he did, and make it thicker. Stevie Wonder did it, most obviously in the song "Saturn." Musically, so did Alice Coltrane, Miles Davis when he went electric, and Herbie Hancock as he experimented with synthesizers. Even Earth, Wind & Fire and The 5th Dimension played with science fiction themes. Perhaps most important, you can hear it, and see it, all over Parliament-Funkadelic, who, in a streak of work that spanned the 1970s—from *Mothership Connection* and *Funkentelechy vs. the Placebo Syndrome* to *Cosmic Slop* and *One Nation Under a Groove* and beyond—took Sun Ra's ideas and ran as far with them as they could. It's not just their outrageous costumes, or their cover art, at once playful and disorienting. Like Sun Ra, P. Funk talks about alienation and liberation, with a lot more emphasis on the latter, and from album to album builds up a complex mythology and cast of characters that draws heavily from comics, cartoons, and especially science fiction. The singers ride atop music that is often dizzyingly complex, yet immediately accessible, because P. Funk never forgot to make it ridiculously fun and ferociously groovy. If Sun Ra made the formula, you could say that P. Funk brought it to the masses.

After P. Funk, it's all over. Parliament-Funkadelic is one of the most sampled bands in hip hop, and lots of artists have explicitly followed in P. Funk's footsteps, marrying science fiction to music and carrying the themes of alienation and liberation still further, from Afrika Bambaataa and Del the Funky Homosapien to OutKast and Kelis. And while Sun Ra was considered on the fringes of jazz when he began—on his own musical planet—science fiction has become much more mainstream in black music since then. Michael Jackson visited it a few times in the second half of his career, and Jay-Z, Beyoncé, Rihanna, and Kayne West are no strangers to the genre. The long-running thread that Sun Ra unspooled is thicker than ever, fat enough to walk on. Like a tightrope. Which is where Janelle Monáe comes in.

> *I-I-I-I-I I'm an alien from outer space*
> *I'm a cyber girl without a face . . .*
> —from "Violet Stars Happy Hunting!"

These are the first words we hear Janelle Monáe sing on her first release, the 2007 EP *Metropolis*. Those *I*s are sung almost like they're record scratches, but also like she's powering up. From the first second, the music is tightly wound and the alienation so strong that the forces gathering against the singer are almost genocidal: "I'm a slave girl without a race," she sings, "on the run 'cause they're here to erase and chase out my kind." The song plunges us into an elaborate backstory described in the album's liner notes. It's the year 2719, and after five world wars and ecological catastrophe, only one city remains, called Metropolis. The debt to Fritz Lang is acknowledged loudly, as Monáe's Metropolis is a place of decadent haves and desperate have-nots, with the twist that the conflicts aren't just between classes, but ethnicities and cultures. It's a rough place. But like the mythological New York that exists in songs and movies, people still keep coming, because Metropolis just happens to be one of those places where, even after the collapse of civilization, you can still make it big.

Monáe's persona in this world is an android named Cindi Mayweather with a "rock-star proficiency package and a working soul." This makes her a fantastic performer, cutting-edge to the point of revolution; it also leads her to break the rules of Metropolis dictating that "androids shall never know love—especially with a human," as she, a have-not, falls in love with a have, Anthony Greendown, "with the eyes of the world watching her." This crime, by Metropolis law, is a capital offense, and as word spreads of what Mayweather has done, she goes on the run, into hiding, underground, pursued by bounty hunters, aliens, and ghosts intent on killing her, even as she becomes a symbol for the have-nots in Metropolis for everything that's wrong with the city's system and what can be done to overcome it.

As mentioned above, the name of Monáe's last human city is totally intentional. When asked about her use of science fiction, she told *Bust* in July 2013 that:

> I would always watch *The Twilight Zone* with my grandmother, and I knew about *Star Wars* and things. But when I met [my producing partners] Chuck Lightning and Nate Wonder, they got me into Isaac Asimov, artificial intelligence, and cybernetics. Chuck asked me to watch *Metropolis,* and I was like, *wow.* I saw the parallels between growing up in Kansas City and the have-nots living underground, working for the haves. That constant struggle was something I could identify with because my parents worked day and night, trying to make a living. I thought science fiction was a great way of talking about the future. It doesn't make people feel like you're talking about things that are happening right now, so they don't feel like you're talking down to them. It gives the listener a different perspective.

The dark world and tension within it that Monáe creates fuels not only *Metropolis: The Chase Suite,* but (so far) all Monáe's output, 2010's *The ArchAndroid* and 2013's *The Electric Lady,* which expand on and elaborate the story, drawing in references to Philip K. Dick and James Cameron's *Terminator* films—her antecedents in dealing with androids—along the way. In the science-fiction world, she knows she's standing on some big shoulders, and she's taken on more material from the genre than most of her musical predecessors. Her contribution, to music and to science fiction, and following Stevie Wonder and Parliament, is to balance the heaviness of the material with some of the fleetest, most joyful, and most uplifting music being written in the pop idiom today.

It begins with Monáe's voice, an instrument that seems to be able to do nearly anything she wants it to do. She can coo and swing, belt it out, screech when she needs to; she can do a melisma with the best of them, but knows when to hit the notes square, too. She has great flow when she raps. Pulling the versatility together is Monáe's energetic delivery, sometimes coiled, sometimes unleashed, but always present, and a lead vocal like that gives Monáe, Chuck Lightning, and Nate Wonder the chance to create arrangements that follow suit. Everything moves, textures shift, instruments switch out from song to song and sometimes within songs. The music bristles with the same restless intelligence that drives Monáe. It bursts with ideas, and at the same time, it is deeply funky.

It's fun to analyze, but it's even more fun to dance to, and Monáe's approach has earned her both fans and rapturous reviews. Writing for Pitchfork, Matthew Perpetua called *The ArchAndroid* "about as bold as mainstream music gets . . . . The first listen is mostly about being wowed by the very existence of this fabulously talented young singer and her over-the-top record; every subsequent spin reveals the depths of her achievement." Jayson Greene called *Electric Lady* "a show-stopping display of force and talent." "Behold," Michael Cregg stated of *The ArchAndroid* in *The Guardian*, "pop music has found its latest superstar"; Alexis Petridis wrote that "at its best, *The Electric Lady* is audacious, intrepid, and brilliantly executed." She has found fans within the science fiction community as well. Writer and music critic Jason Heller calls her "one of the most important artists in pop right now"; "what I love most about her style," he says, "is the swaggering sureness of her belief that SF can be written, and written well, in any medium imaginable." Writer Daniel José Older says that "*ArchAndroid* and *Electric Lady* incorporate so many elements we spec fic writers strive for: world building, character development, inner and outer conflicts, sharp social and political analysis, escalating moods and movements, violent crossroads of the future and past . . . As writers, we could learn a lot from Janelle Monáe."

Striking the balance isn't always easy, though, and Monáe has had her detractors. She's been called overly ambitious; writing in *Rolling Stone* about *Electric Lady*, Jon Dolan argued that "you've got to admire an artist who can cut through the weight of her own pretensions," but then nonetheless stated that "with Janelle Monáe, the pretensions are pretty impressive"—and this was in a positive review. Declaring *The ArchAndroid* to be "the most overrated album of the year," Robert Christgau said of Monáe that "all she can do well is dance—her songwriting is 60th percentile, her singing technical, her sci-fi plot the usual rot." Jody Rosen declared *Electric Lady* to be "an intermittently thrilling failure," and regarding her use of science fiction, he saw "nothing much of interest in Monáe's muddled story line—certainly none of the eerie tragicomedy of Sun Ra and P. Funk's space explorations." Writing in *Slate* about *The*

ArchAndroid—and the following statement is a little weird, since, unless there are two music critics named Jody Rosen, he gave the album a generally positive review in *Rolling Stone*—he stated further that:

> Monáe [and Erykah Badu] . . . want to be geniuses, and they want to do it the easy way, by shortcut—by tossing together Afro-futurist theology, '70s soul, and other hallowed styles and signifiers, and insisting that it all adds up to something transcendent. It pains me that so many smart critics have fallen for music that's so slapdash and self-impressed.

"What am I missing?" he asked.

> *When you get elevated*
> *They love it or they hate it*
> *You dance up on them haters*
> *Keep getting funky on the scene*
> —from "Tightrope"

The response of Janelle Monáe's predecessors to the themes of alienation and liberation has been a kind of all-out exuberance, from Sun Ra's polyphony to P. Funk's non-stop party. It's not just in the music, either; it's in the lyrics, the stage persona, the costumes that let the audience know, in no uncertain terms, that they are dealing with a person from another planet, even if it's just a metaphor. They explore the themes together, and push them out.

Monáe's move, though certainly exuberant, is different. As Jayson Greene said in Pitchfork, "her music has always been about the exhilaration coming from the sensation of total control." The songs are full of energy, but never wild; tightly coiled, never slack. Her contribution— musically and thematically—is to place alienation and liberation against one another in a way not quite done before, and then to balance her work directly on the tension between them. This balance, for Monáe, is personal, artistic, even political. When Nisha Gopalan asked Monáe in Vulture about her father's substance abuse and how it shaped her, she responded:

> Well, first, my father is clean. He's sober. He had hard time. I was able to see firsthand what drugs do. I learned a lot from my dad. I learned how to be resilient, how to not hold on to the past. He's so much better, and I'm so proud of him: where's

he's been, where he comes from, and where he is now. And it also made me want to write music. I was really inspired by the highs and lows of life. In this industry, there's so many highs and lows. So I have to remain balanced, with my head held high.

And before performing for Barack Obama in support of his reelection in 2012, she stated:

I wrote "Tightrope" because it talks about dealing with balance—don't get too high, don't get too low. And that's one of the things that I've noticed about President Obama.

This personal, aesthetic, and political use of balance points toward a way forward, not only for Monáe as she continues to develop her work, but for fellow musicians and science-fiction creators. As Heller says, "there aren't many authors working right now who seem to understand that they can marry a sense of adventure, kinetic crackle, and giddy fun to all the stoic, weighty conceptual stuff." Monáe is doing it; we can, too. All we have to do is do it.

So when Rosen says that Monáe "wants to be a genius," he isn't so much "missing" something as reading too much into it. So am I, in this essay, when I freight her music with all this abstract rhetorical baggage. Monáe may get down, but she's also just getting to work. She's not just making a fashion statement by always appearing in a tuxedo. It's her uniform. As she said at a BET awards ceremony,

When I started my music career, I was a maid. I used to clean houses. My mother was a proud janitor. My stepfather, who raised me like his very own, worked at the post office and my father was a trashman. They all wore uniforms and that's why I stand here today, in my black and white, and I wear my uniform to honor them. This is a reminder that I have work to do. I have people to uplift. I have people to inspire.

And it works. As Nora Jemisin writes,

It's easy to look at something like Monáe's mythos and see only the obvious metaphors . . . . But it's wrong to apply only an historical, and racial, lens to the work of any modern black woman. We have spent generations sharing the struggles of other oppressed groups, collaborating with and occasionally being betrayed by them, and progressing nonetheless.

As dystopian as the albums' backstory is, Jemisin continues,

> It's clear that Monáe feels no sense of threat from the others with whom our future will be shared. She welcomes all, with love and dancing . . . . I'm not sure this future is the kind of place I'd want to live in, but I definitely wouldn't mind visiting. And for as long as Janelle Monáe is willing to offer my imagination this kind of gleeful romp, I'll keep coming back.

When she hears "Tightrope," she says, "I can't listen to [it] without dancing. I'm a terrible dancer but I don't care. I lose myself in it because Monáe's magic is for everybody."

Monáe's just working, and it works. Which might be the most inspiring thing of all.

ABOUT THE AUTHOR

Brian Francis Slattery is an editor, writer, and author of four novels, the third of which won the Philip K. Dick Award. He lives in New Haven, CT.

Science Fiction Writers Wear Disguises: A Conversation with Robert Reed

ALVARO ZINO-AMARO

Robert Reed was born at the height of the Eisenhower administration, in Omaha, Nebraska. Growing up a few miles from the Strategic Air Command, he realized early and often that the world balances on a razor. His fiction mirrors that sense of bleak amazement. Hundreds of stories and more than a dozen novels have led to numerous award nominations, and Reed won one Hugo Award, for his novella, "A Billion Eves."

He lives today in Lincoln, Nebraska with his wife and daughter, and he has no escape plan in case of nuclear war.

I've known him since 2008 and he reports that, since then, his running has gotten a little slower—but happily for me and all the other readers who enjoy his work, his writing pace hasn't decreased at all. I interviewed him in 2009, and he fictionalized our meeting in his story "Excellence" (*Asimov's*, December 2010), in which I became Gilchrist, whom the narrator describes as "shorter than I would have guessed, wearing what looked like a fresh shirt and slacks and a decidedly bland tie." This time I skipped the formal attire.

In 2013 you published The Greatship, a collection of stories you linked with newly written "bridges," as you called them. Can you talk a little about these bridges and the process of selecting and ordering these stories?

Bridges, yeah, that was my term. I've trademarked that. Anytime anyone uses the term "bridge," now I get a small royalty.

The first bridges were built for *Marrow* (2000), and they weren't intended to serve the function they ended up serving in other works. But basically, for a big book like this, I would try to give some background. And the point of view ended up eventually becoming that of the Great Ship. That wasn't clear to me in *Marrow*, but by *The Well of Stars* (2004) I was definitely doing the voice of the Great Ship. And I felt that when you have all these stories that, frankly, aren't well linked with one another, it was best to have some overriding principle or presence. I liked the process of writing the bridges a lot. They were fun to write, which is not a bad thing.

As for the ordering of the stories, that right there is an element of guesswork. There is no clear existing chronology for this work. I don't have some calendar where I keep track of what happens where. We're talking about over a hundred thousand years of history. I started with "Alone," which was a novella, because it seemed to be the perfect opening for the broader story. It begins at the beginning, and ends kind of in the middle of what you might see as the history of the Great Ship.

So can we now take the order of the stories in this collection as a rough chronology?

Yes, you can. But don't bet any great sums of money on it staying the same.

Well, you've mentioned that The Greatship will be an evolving project, where new material is added to the old in successive iterations. What made you decide to take this approach rather than, say, putting out additional story collections?

This is digital, so it can be a huge volume. Size is not an issue. And I think if you're really interested in the subject of the Great Ship, this is a very good way to figure out my head, or as close as you're going to get. Because I will make decisions that may change things. I could change the order, for example, because I find a better first story. I don't think I will—but I might. I might also rewrite the bridge material; I don't know. This is a problem I'll attack if and when I get there. If you want the new stories, you'll need to buy the old stories all over again, yes, but that's why I'm only asking $4.99 for the ebook. I've actually been surprised by how many people have bought the physical edition, because I don't think it looks great, but it's had some sales, so I'm pleased with that.

Your latest Great Ship work, The Memory of Sky (2014), was a trilogy published all at once. How did that come about?

There's a long history here. The first novel, *Diamond*, was written several years ago, after a sort of powwow with a couple of editors that suggested I try a YA approach. So I tried YA, in the sense that I had a young protagonist, and thought the story would be interesting for kids. I kept away from sex, and I kept away from hugely overt violence, but it was still my story, basically a wonderland I built for this boy. It then sat with an editor at Tor, who really liked it, but who unfortunately couldn't sell it to the bosses that be. I revised it. Then my agent and I ended up negotiating with Amazon. Their contract was peculiar. The legal department at my agent's house was okay with it, but it was a bizarre contract, in that it didn't seem to spell out the kinds of things that normally get spelled out in contracts. I was very close to signing it, and was even going to get an advance from them—which I hear is unusual—but then I asked who, hypothetically, was going to be my editor. And they said, "Oh, you want an editor?" At that point I thought, "Maybe this isn't such a good idea."

Then I got an online nibble—well, more than a nibble—from Prime Books. And they wanted a trilogy, which is what I started to write. At Prime Books I felt free to do what I wanted. My original story, the first novel, was open-ended, and it was a massive advantage now to have time and look again at what I had written. I'm always sober, but I was even more sober, or unsentimental, about what I'd done. Now I was looking for a certain way of telling the story that could be elaborated into other tales further down. I had to put the story in a location that would serve later stories. I had to start thinking about the Great Ship as a place, and defining what it is and what it isn't. I had to start thinking in timescales that were a bit different from what I had before. Once I figured all that out, I was able to start working on the other books.

The original publishing plan was to have each book come out every six months or so. But Barnes & Noble was concerned that doing it that way they'd get good sales on the first, but that then things would taper. So they asked us, "Could you do it all as one volume?" Now there was an upper size limit, and a tighter deadline for the third book. This is an example of a situation where a writer has to juggle several balls at once. I had created requirements in my story, like all the characters being together in one place in one day during the final book. But I had to compress the material, still keeping to that. It turned out that the size limitation was an enormous blessing. I wrote it fairly quickly, with a pretty clear picture of where I was going. Occasionally things happened that I didn't expect, and I really enjoyed that. The second book is the longest of the three. The tone also changes from the first book to the second one; things get darker. My wife noticed that when she read the trilogy.

I like writing because it's like super-reading. I've said that before, and I'll always say it. When I'm involved in my writing, it makes reading seem like a pretty prosaic walk in the park. This was intense for me. I had a general sense of what I wanted to happen, but no outline. I bounced some characters off each other. I didn't know one character would be suicidal until I started writing the third book. But there she is. That was one of the bigger surprises. You start looking at your people, and you see the world through their eyes. I try to understand their point of view. A long time ago my agent said that with her clients, she could tell from their stories what some of their opinions were. But with me she can't.

Will there be more Great Ship novels/trilogies? Any involving the character of Diamond?

Yes. Since *The Memory of Sky* came out I've been working hard in my head. I don't do outlines but in this case I wrote some stuff down—there's now an actual file! But it's just a general sense of things, of what I want this world to be like. I'm not pretending to say, "This happens in that chapter." During all these months of work I've learned a lot more about the Great Ship, and ways of presenting things. The reader won't know what's happening right away, and I will push that as far as I can. I have a new trilogy in mind. The working title is *The Dragons of Marrow*. There are nine dragons, and they aren't what you think they are. I came up with this scheme—when I figured it out—it was like, "Man!"

You continue to be a prolific short story writer. Several of your recent stories revolve around the Fermi paradox. One of them, "Aether," is in the anthology Paradox, edited by Ian Whates. What are some of the others, and what inspired you to write them?

At WorldCon I was on a panel about colonizing other worlds. There were three world scenarios we were supposed to talk about: Mars or a Mars-like world, a living world without any sentient life, and a living world with low-technology sentient life. What should we do if we came across these worlds? I pointed out that we've been living in a solar system where for four-point-five billion years, each of these scenarios has been true at some point. Mars has been open territory for anyone to come and make it into a habitable place. From what we can see, no one has. Earth has been habitable to some sort of life—if not always human—for several billion years. And in the last few hundred years, we've made a lot of noise and have built industrial products that are noticeable at a distance. All of those things have happened, but no one is here, no one is renovating. Which makes me wonder: where are they?

It's not just me. A lot of very serious people are wondering. But I'm not sure that in science fiction we care that much. It's the game: we need to tell stories. But the reality is that going from star to star is extremely hard work, and life may not be the answer, etc. etc. There's many options. "wHole" is a recent story that examines some of these issues. The best way I can describe the story, is that apparently I do a lot of drugs. "What I Intend," currently under submission, is another. And right now I'm working on another, called "Empty." This is the fourth scenario I've come up with for the Fermi paradox. I try to imagine novel answers. It's a fascinating question, because the universe should be full of life, kicking us around, passing through us, whatever. And it isn't.

Can you talk a little about your video-game related writing for the game Destiny? Your website mentions a forthcoming story related to the game, called "What Remains."

This has been a very different experience for me, because it's not my universe, and because I have people who are very interested in what I write every step of the way, virtually. "What Remains" is something I wrote for them a couple of years ago, but has since been retooled a few times, once by me, and once by them, split up and used for various things in game. Or said differently, inside the game there will be some of my words. I wrote it in the second person, and they let me keep it that way, which was nice.

Bungie, the makers of *Destiny*, gave me certain guiding points, and a certain terminology that might be very valuable for me to know. I was able to watch some of the video sequences and make notes, though my notes are always largely incomprehensible. I also asked them what I thought were basic story questions, and sometimes the answer would be, "We haven't figured that out yet," or "We don't have bandwidth for that." They have a history for the game worlds, but they also have gaps. Last time I was in Seattle, I tried to play the game. I'm bad with games. Basically they had to make me invincible so I could march my way through the game's beautiful landscape to achieve the ending. So I got to see how things should be.

Can you talk a little about your decision to self-publish short stories on your blog Reshaping Light?

There are four out so far, "Carnage," "Far-farfetched," "Khan," and "One City." *Reshaping Light* is a blog I started up so I could bitch about movies, go into what I don't like about them. I think modern movies are extremely pretty to watch but are oftentimes just dumb stories, truly stupid stories, *imbecilic* stories—am I making my point clear here? Just basic crap that doesn't make sense at all. Characters that are arbitrary and pulled out of stock, and so on. Many of these movies are simple, ugly things that are brought up into the digital light of day for a while and then fade. There's a lot of explosions. Young men and their dates will watch them.

So what I wanted to do was find stories that were reasonably interesting, or that at least I would find interesting, based on movies I watched. *Iron Man 3* had this one story arc I didn't care for, and a true villain that wasn't compelling at all. I remember thinking that they should have started with that final fight sequence. I liked the part where his girlfriend became a superhero—but how would that affect their relationship? Ultimately I wasn't thrilled with my own way of handling things either, but I wanted to at least attempt a storyline instead of just bitching about it.

Basically each of these stories rewrites a movie, but I don't tell you which movie it is. You can figure it out if you've seen the source material.

There's more to come in this project. I really enjoyed *Margin Call*—a wonderful movie. It's about the financial collapse. But I think if you could rewrite it, it would be the perfect way to talk about the singularity. A bunch of nerds sitting around, and instead of thinking, "Hmm, these numbers don't make sense," they realize, "We have something here. *Something's* happening." Approach it with the same tone, with good-looking actors, and it would be wonderful! This one isn't so much a bitch session, but the thought that this movie would be a great vehicle for other things.

Any other projects not related to the Great Ship, commissioned stories for anthologies, Bungie, or rewriting movies?

I would like to talk about a book I've been working on for years in various forms. It's a mammoth book. The book is about three hundred and seventy thousand words of daily life in a deeply alternate world. But it focuses mostly on what you eat, where you go to work, and sex.

So you've invented a new genre—not the alternate novella, but the alternate novela, as in telenovela.

Yes, that's my invention! As mentioned, this a big project. My agent's looking for a home for it. A piece of it was published as "The Principles" in *Asimov's*, though to a kind of lukewarm response. I have a second story I've also pulled from the book, which now doesn't end in the same way as it does in the novel, and I'd like to sell that too. Ideally I'd like to sell the whole book. I enjoyed writing it, enjoyed rewriting it, and will probably enjoy rewriting it again before it's published. But at some point, even if I have to do it myself, it will be published.

It's had a number of titles, like *The World of My Brother*, and *Pussyworld*; it depends on my mood. I remember once Garrison Keillor talking about a writer's life, back when he was doing the poem of the day bit on PBS, which we get in Lincoln. He was talking about Chuck Palahniuk, the author of *Fight Club*. The manuscript for that novel was being rejected. Apparently it was offending people. There were two directions Palahniuk thought he should go: he could dilute it down, or make it worse, push the material harder. He went the latter way. That made me think, "How would I do that with this story?" And that's where I am today.

Alvaro Zino-Amaro is the co-author, with Robert Silverberg, of *When the Blue Shift Comes,* which received a starred review from *Library Journal.* Alvaro's short fiction and poetry have appeared or are forthcoming in *Analog, Nature, Galaxy's Edge, Apex* and other venues, and Alvaro was nominated for the 2013 Rhysling Award. Alvaro's reviews, critical essays and interviews have appeared in *The Los Angeles Review of Books, Strange Horizons, SF Signal, The New York Review of Science Fiction, Foundation,* and other markets. Alvaro currently edits the blog for *Locus.*

Another Word:
What You Know

DANIEL ABRAHAM

One of the many, many times I started figuring out how to write fiction, I was early in my college career. I had a couple of resources: creative writing classes and how-to-write books whose titles I will omit here out of an abundance of charity. One of the things that I found back then was a lot of pithy truism meant to guide the aspiring writer that carried a weight usually reserved for scripture: Show, Don't Tell; Write What You Know; and so on.

As I've gone on, I've gone from clinging to these to being skeptical of almost all of them. The one that took the longest to fall from grace with me was Show, Don't Tell. It turns out that being able to write summary narrative is really important, evoking the physical sensations of everything can get just as dull as exposition, and knowing when to do which one is a critical skill. But I digress.

As with so many things, though, there's an exception. I rejected Write What You Know pretty much in the time it took to hear the last syllable. It took me years to find an interpretation of those words that actually made sense.

The truth is, I don't really know when someone first told me Write What You Know, but given where I was at the time, I can speculate. I took creative writing classes when I was in school, usually because it was a quick three credits of A. The system was always pretty much the same: a class full of college-age students under the guidance of a teacher who—with few and memorable exceptions—didn't earn a living writing fiction. We met in the classroom, read one another's work, and told each other what was and wasn't working in hopes that in aggregate, we were smarter, more sophisticated, more insightful and more nurturing of literary talent than any of us were individually.

I've got no stones to throw here. I'm sure there are worse ways to teach, but the skills *I* learned were about how to get along well in that kind of class: how to express my opinions—however ill-founded—with confidence; how to offer criticism that sounded a lot like the five people who went before me without quite copying them; how to amend my opinion of a piece of work when it became clear the room—and especially the teacher—disagreed with me. The truth is, those classes were easy and fun. I liked them. But somewhere in there, someone trotted out the idea that you should Write What You Know, and like any good speculative fiction writer, I rolled my eyes and dismissed it.

Because, *really*, had Frank Herbert lived on Arrakis? Had Le Guin summered in Earthsea as a child? Writing what you knew seemed to me like a backhanded way of saying don't write fantastika. And it *was* used to mean that sometimes. The prejudice against what I do was certainly part of the academic water in which I swam. I understand from those who are younger or who have more of a taste for that kind of thing, it still is. As a motto for championing strictly mimetic fiction and encouraging more stories about being an undergraduate, it's dumb.

But an interesting thing happens when you distill an aesthetic insight into a bumper sticker. The same words can have several meanings.

A few years ago, I had dinner with Junot Díaz who in addition to being a passionate and brilliant author also teaches creative writing in an academic setting. We didn't talk about the rule to Write What You Know, but we did talk about how people teach writing and how they learn it. Junot told me that, in his experience, playwrights in the theater departments know more about structure and storytelling than the creative writers in English departments. After that, the conversation moved on to the role-playing systems we'd all preferred as kids, but that idea stuck with me, and—after having published six or seven novels—I started the process of learning to write. I do that pretty much every three or four years.

Lajos Egri published the first version of *The Art of Dramatic Writing* in 1942. The copy I have is the 54th edition. In it, he spends a lot of space talking about the idea of premise. I can't do his argument justice in a few sentences, so I'll just give you two aspects of the discussion that struck home for me.

First, there's the idea of starting with a premise. The premise of a story (according to Egri's analysis) is like one of the morals for Aesop. It's the argument the story makes. So, for example, Egri says the premise of Othello is "Jealousy destroys itself and the object of its love." For

Ibsen's *Ghosts:* "The sins of the father are visited on the children." Now, working more than seven decades after the book first saw print, I have some quibbles about the role of the audience versus the vision of the artist, but okay. Whatever. I didn't have the same experience of some of the plays that Egri did. Also fine. Put that aside.

The other thing that Egri said—one of the many other things —is that it's very hard and maybe impossible to write a good, solid story based in a premise you don't believe. That struck home.

I have been in critique groups since college, and some of them have been very, very good, especially the ones that included professional writers who took their craft seriously. I have learned a tremendous amount about how to do what I do. And one thing I've seen over and over is how a story comes alive when it *matters* to the author.

I didn't—and still don't—begin anything I do with Egri's premise theory in mind. But I've learned to see what it is in each project I do that I would champion. I try to lean into those arguments and thoughts and ideas. I try to cut out the bits that get in the way. Usually, they weren't working anyway. I've written things that, in retrospect, I can see premises in like "Love alone offers no safety" and "Holding on to a failed relationship leads to debasement" and—more often than anything else "Simplistic morality leads to atrocity." All of those speak to my experience.

And so I cycled back to Write What You Know.

When someone uses that phrase to talk about the concrete details of a particular life—implying that middle-class college undergrads shouldn't write about fantasy kings and queens, high school students should only write about high school, Anglos should only write about Anglos, straight people about straight people, men about men, women about women—it's a small, stupid, venal argument. It's immoral, and more than that, it's bad craft.

On the other hand, when we use it (as I choose to) to mean Write What You Know *To Be True*— write work that, regardless of the setting or the characters or the plot, is based in the sense you've made of the world, is informed by the insights you've had about what it is to be human, has (in Egri's terms) a premise you believe—it's more than just good advice.

It's a statement about the morality of art, because it means that living a full life, building a deep understanding of the world and our place in it, cultivating—however imperfectly—*wisdom* is an issue of good craftsmanship.

ABOUT THE AUTHOR

Daniel Abraham is a writer of genre fiction with a dozen books in print and over thirty published short stories. His work has been nominated for the Nebula, World Fantasy, and Hugo Awards and has been awarded the International Horror Guild Award. He also writes as MLN Hanover and (with Ty Franck) as James S. A. Corey. He lives in the American Southwest.

Editor's Desk:
Eight Is a Good Number
NEIL CLARKE

Despite the October-inspired darker tone of this issue, things have been going very well here at *Clarkesworld*. This issue marks our eighth anniversary and I have all sorts of good news to share. It's hard to decide where to start, so I'm just going to do this in chronological order.

In early September, we won the British Fantasy Award for Best Magazine/ Periodical at a ceremony held during FantasyCon in York, UK. Sadly, we weren't able to be there in person, but I did send along a video just in case. We'd like to thank the members of BSFA for their nominations and the judges for the honor they've bestowed on us. This is our first British Fantasy Award win and we're completely blown away by this news.

If you like cyborgs, you should check out my recent anthology *Upgraded*. It was published in trade paperback and ebook editions in September and has been receiving some very nice reviews. Initial orders were strong enough that the book almost immediately went into a second printing, which should hit the shelves mid-month. Looking for a first edition? Barnes & Noble ordered the most copies so they should still have some or you can buy direct from Wyrm Publishing. The ebook editions are available in all the usual places. By the way, E. Catherine Tobler's story in this issue is a companion piece to her story in *Upgraded*.

In last month's editorial, I announced our plans to regularly publish translated stories from China. Our Kickstarter campaign, which is still ongoing as I write this, has successfully funded the first year of this project, and we are hoping to include the first of many stories in our 100th issue this January. This means that our 2015 issues will be bigger than ever and feature four or five original works in each issue.

The response to our Kickstarter campaign was so enthusiastic that it funded in its first week. I'm very pleased that so many people are interested in reading more international science fiction represented in our pages, and to that end, we announced a Kickstarter stretch goal that will build a translation fund that will allow us to occasionally feature stories translated from even more languages. Again, this would be a supplemental story and not replace any of our regular fiction slots. We won't know if this extra project will happen until after October 8, so I'll give you another update next month.

Finally, we would like to congratulate Xia Jia. Last month, we published "Spring Festival: Happiness, Anger, Love, Sorrow, Joy" translated by Ken Liu. Ken has informed us that the original version of the story is one of five nominees for the Chinese Nebula Award. This is one of two highest honors that can be given in China, the other being the Galaxy Award. We're very proud to have published the English language edition and wish her the best of luck!

ABOUT THE AUTHOR

Neil Clarke is the editor of *Clarkesworld Magazine,* owner of Wyrm Publishing and a current Hugo Award Nominee for Best Editor (short form). He currently lives in NJ with his wife and two children.

About the Artist

SANDEEP KARUNAKARAN

Sandeep Karunakaran is a self-taught science fiction and fantasy artist from Calicut (Kerala) in the southern part of India. He started drawing at a very early age and always had a keen interest in paintings, cartoons, and comics. Sandeep originally focused on traditional painting and made the leap to digital in 2002. He approaches his work as visual storytelling and incorporates a full-spectrum of themes from scientific exploration to dark disturbing nightmares.

WEBSITE

sanskarans.deviantart.com